Praise for Dan O'Brien

A Story That Happens

"A master class in surviving through art."

Margaret Gray, *The Los Angeles Times*

"Powerful . . . . This is a book for our times. It reminds us that theatre is 'fractured and failing yet struggling towards the mouth's translation of the heart's tongue'. Like [O'Brien], we buzz with the desire for the 'chance for more life, and for that most valued of theatrical currencies – change'."

Alice Jolly, *The Times Literary Supplement*

"Subtly weaving between sometimes harrowing personal reminiscences and perceptive and astute lessons on the art of dramatic writing, the book is a quiet revelation."

Caridad Svich, *Contemporary Theatre Review*

Our Cancers

"*Our Cancers* is an excellent example of Shelley's secret alchemy, that turns 'to potable gold the poisonous waters which flow from death through life.' . . . Writing the truth, [O'Brien] says, 'saved him.' And it has produced an exquisite and terrible beauty in these pages."

Steven Wilson, *The Times Literary Supplement*

"O'Brien explains that his obligation as a writer is 'To tell the truth as skillfully as possible. To make art out of pain. To heal.' *Our Cancers* tells his truth not only skillfully but masterfully, making from pain a lasting chronicle of art that traces fragmentary moments of healing over time."

J.D. Schraffenberger, *North American Review*

Also by Dan O'Brien

Prose

*A Story That Happens: On Playwriting, Childhood,
& Other Traumas*

Poetry

Survivor's Notebook
Our Cancers
New Life
Scarsdale
War Reporter

Plays

True Story: A Trilogy
The Angel in the Trees and Other Monologues
The House in Scarsdale
The Body of an American
Dan O'Brien: Plays One

Dan O'Brien

FROM SCARSDALE

a childhood

DALKEY ARCHIVE PRESS
Dallas / Dublin

ISBN (pb): 978-1-62897-548-2 | ISBN (ebook): 978-1-62897-553-6
Library of Congress Cataloging-in-Publication Data: Available.

Interior design by Anuj Mathur
Cover design by Anna Jordan

Dalkey Archive Press
www.dalkeyarchive.com
Dallas, TX / Rochester, NY

Printed on permanent/durable acid-free paper.

for my family

Table of Contents

HE WAS STUMBLING around the side of the house, no jacket, no shoes. Was he barefoot? The seat of his jeans, the shoulders and back of his blue wool sweater, his mussed blond hair all matted with snow, melting against the glass of the storm door as he struggled to open the front door. The pineapple-shaped brass knocker glinted with each jerk. As we pulled into the driveway I pointed him out to our mother.

She followed him inside. Slumped at the breakfast table in slanted winter sunlight, he was crying—no, sobbing. Convulsively. I'd never heard such sounds before. She knelt with her hand on his knee. "What did you do?" she asked him, over and over. Then to me without looking: "Take your sister upstairs."

Joyce was away at college; this was her vacated attic bedroom where I sat on the floor beside my younger sister Sally as she played with her dolls. How much time had passed? Steven appeared out of nowhere, holding baby Tommy in his arms: "Paul jumped off the roof," he said, as if sharing some delicious gossip, and our mother was driving him to Dr. Linden.

But the roof? How could he have climbed up there? He must have been sick; I'd seen him coughing through his tears, his chest and neck straining for breath. Suddenly I was certain I would get sick too, would catch his disease, whatever it was. On the way up the stairs I had noticed that the window in our

11

father's attic office was gone, removed from its quarter-moon frame and laid on the floor against the wall. A screwdriver and some screws were scattered across the desk, beside a note scribbled on loose-leaf. "Dear Mom: Looks like you'll finally get that playroom you've always wanted."

She'd been pressuring him for months to move up to the attic. Her second-born, her eldest son, had grown into a disappointment that she seemed to want only to forget, to exile him to the room where I was now, unaware that I might never truly leave this room again, might never stop trying to understand what was happening to my brother and to us all.

That night, when my mother came home, I led her up to the attic. Our father was at the hospital still, the hospital where we'd been born; Paul had been "shaking like a leaf" when she left his bedside, Mother said. I handed her the note and watched her read and she collapsed crying in my arms.

"This is a secret," she whispered, her breath in my ear, "we must take to our graves."

When I was forty-two years old a softball-sized tumor was cut out of my colon. *This has been a long time coming*, I thought as I lay in the hospital bed. Perhaps the cancer had been growing in me since that Tuesday afternoon in February in 1986 when my brother tried to kill himself. He was seventeen and I was twelve. And from that day on I had symptoms, brought on by stress. My mother's reassuringly dismissive diagnosis—"spastic colon, the curse of the O'Briens"—kept me from the doctor sooner. (Though the blame, if there must be blame, is mine.) Had the tumor been growing for thirty years, fed by my ambition, my masochism, my writing? Had it metastasized like a singularly scarring memory I could not or would not forget?

Six months earlier my wife had been diagnosed with a

mid-stage breast cancer. Our daughter was not yet two. I knew that now was the right time, the only time, to begin to tell the truth of my childhood. To understand why ours was a tragic family. To try to cure myself for my family—my family now, my wife and daughter—by writing the story of who I am and where I'm from with honesty, insight, and something like forgiveness. To try to leave the old place behind.

I. Her Ambition

With Her

SHE LAID ME down swaddled upon the snowy skirts of the tree, beneath fragrant needles and glittering multicolored globes, nestled between gift-wrapped boxes as if the Magi had already come and gone. I was her early Christmas gift, she liked to say, as my birthday was exactly three weeks to the day before Jesus's and—though she'd never admit it out loud—I was meant to be her savior.

I was born like, *I'm here, I'm ready.* That's the way my mother told it anyway—and I believe her, having seen my daughter prised from my wife's body, wailing furiously, flopping astride her mother's belly, feeding lustily. "Old soul" is how old women identified me from the start, and now I see why, as my daughter came into this world with my same furrowed brow, my worried wrinkle between her wide, watchful eyes.

On the stairs, tucked between her thighs, in the rocking chair in her bedroom, on the sofa, after the world had drained away into schools and shops and office buildings, I listened to my mother recite nursery rhymes. Her childish voice could almost sing. Mother Goose, Humpty-Dumpty, all the king's horses and lions and unicorns. Poetry was inculcated here; also my distrust of strict meter and rhyme.

I slapped my bare feet through the bars of my crib. When soiled and sodden my cries went unanswered: neglect meant to teach me. I was terrified of the nursery window that looked out on our backyard and that lightning-struck tree with a knot like a mournful face. I confessed my fear to my mother. "You will be a poet," she said to me, maybe for the first time.

The unglimpsable surface of tables. The canine-smelling carpet. Finding friendship with legs, human and wooden, treating shoes as pets. Wind slammed the door and I caterwauled; the door opening in a draft was evidence of the invisible world undisclosed.

I derived my first melancholy from a music box with a red-balled crank and handle. Reeling in my tune like a fisherman, I observed the toy's clockwork guts turning through a window in its plastic shell, as it hauntingly, haltingly eked out the theme from *Swan Lake*.

At some point, and for no reason I could fathom, I found myself soon on the sunny side of the house, where the windows faced our dead-end street, across the hallway from my parents. I would spend the rest of my childhood in this room, where the wallpaper was maritime (clippers and cutters, a salty skipper wrestling his wheel in a squall) and for a while my two older brothers were my bunkmates. How did we all fit in such a confined space? I have no memory of feeling cozy here.

Summer twilight outlining the edges of my bedroom curtains could induce in me a panicked intimation of the death-bed. I never sucked my thumb or fingers, did not cling to blankie or binkie. I was strange; felt special, born with a nevus in the blue of my iris, a raised mole on my check, and a flat one on the inside of my left pointer finger, just where my daughter has hers. My daughter and I have plumpish hands, our knuckles dimple. Our veins are hard to find despite our pale skin. We rash quickly, are prone to warts. Our necks are willowy, or mine used to be: "swanlike," as it was described to me many times, and never as a compliment.

Also like my daughter I did not care for holding hands, preferring instead to accompany my shadow through the deep trenches of blizzarded streets. Across the snow-blanked ballfield I marked my canvas, ice in the heel of my mitten, ice in the heel of my boot, glancing over my shoulder at my parents and siblings, my sparrow tracks like an umbilicus connecting me inescapably to them.

I was normal: a hedonist leaping through sprinklers in neighbors' yards, the soaked grass sucking like sponge between my sunburnt toes; running through the line of scarecrow pines to the Mormons' yard and back again while Mother laid out our lovers' picnic in the dandelions and crabgrass, while our mutt Chipper barked and nipped at my heels.

Like my daughter I stare at everything I cannot see. Especially when I am shy. "You think too much," my daughter, like my mother long ago, likes to tease; and they are right. We dream, my daughter and I. We enter a room with equipoise and purpose, and others seem to want to listen, to follow. As if we are self-possessed. Often enough we are enough unto ourselves.

I catch myself staring at my daughter as my father used to stare at me. I am awestruck, as fathers ought to be, by the clarity of her composite beauty, her exponentially blooming knowledge, the ever-shifting mixture of whom she resembles most in appearance and behavior. Perhaps my father was similarly amazed, as he watched me across the dining room table, though I doubt it. His gaze was confounded and disturbed; he was studying me, searching for the solution to a mystery that predated my birth—that was my birth, in a way. Though decades would pass before it occurred to me to solve this mystery for myself.

Against Him

LIFTING THE HORSESHOE from the sand I clanged its brittle tone against the rusty stake. Motorboats seething, children cannonading off the dock into the lake . . .

I offered the horseshoe to my father where he sat upon the throne of his folding beach chair—then dropped it on his foot. The skin of his ankle flushed, his face purpling with rage, as Mother swept me into the shade of the trees.

I woke myself singing and sang myself to sleep. Mother called this unconscious compulsion my "ya-yas," because "ya-ya" was my lyric in toto, repeatedly if variably syncopated, as I flexed and clicked my jaw in an anxious improvisation of melody.

Father hated my singing, and many mornings I awoke to his tasseled penny loafer, or his wingtip with the dime-size hole in its sole, sailing through my open door and walloping off the wall—"Shut up!"

Or I'd open my eyes in the night to Mother's distraught face, her fingernails raking my arm, pinching and twisting my skin, as she whipped the blanket aside and jerked me up in bed and pulled my bottoms down to spank my buttocks, while Steven feigned sleep in the bed opposite. I was singing again soon enough; I couldn't help it. "You must be quiet," she'd whisper—pleading now—"or your father will come in here next."

In the daylight she told us fairy tales: "Your father is not an ogre. Why do you all think of him that way? If you think he's bad, you should have met my mother . . ." But our father *was* an ogre—that's exactly what he was to his children.

I crawled on the floor at his feet in the living room one sweltering summer night. In his yellowed briefs and undershirt in the flickering TV light, he lifted a stack of newspapers over his head—like Moses ready to smash his commandments, or Yahweh Himself to smite another sinner—before slamming it down beside my face. I cried like a baby. I'd been in the way.

If I threw tantrums, I can't remember. When my friends raged and wailed in their homes, at their parents' feet, I cringed with shame for them, and for myself.

In my socks with my shoes in my hands I raced upstairs. He was shouting again. My fingers fumbled to work the laces into any semblance of a knot (I hadn't yet learned how). My mother followed, kneeling beside me: "We have to hurry."

"I hate him," I said. "When will he be dead?"

She paled; she recognized trouble ahead. "You don't know him like I do," she said quietly, tying the laces of my shoes tightly. "He's different when we're alone."

"Mrs. O'Brien"

THEY WERE CHILDREN themselves. My mother Nancy was a junior, younger than her classmates. She had skipped a grade, she would often remind us, thanks to her genius-level IQ. My father Harry was a senior, soon to graduate, and—surprising nobody—he lacked a date for the prom. His older brother John Jr. was friends with my mother's older sister, Ilana, who, like Johnny, was popular; attractive and "wild," according to my mother, soon to march on Washington with MLK and marry a marine, running beneath crossed swords toward her honeymoon car.

My mother's hair was a wiry black frizz. Her face was striking. Her expression, even as a girl, could be severe, with her jutting jaw, a clenched smile exposing a gap between her front teeth—a gap nearly identical to the one between her future husband's front teeth, weirdly.

My father's brother Johnny was a glad-handing, back-slapping football player. "Big man on campus" is how my mother would describe him sardonically. He must have pitied his little brother Harry, with those thick eyeglasses and a predilection for science fiction. So Johnny and Ilana fixed up their sad siblings on a blind date for the prom.

We never heard the story of our father meeting our mother's family. He must have been terrified. He knew they had money; years later he would admit that he had thought they were Jewish. I imagine my pimply father ringing the doorbell of the Welsh family mansion (bestowed with the curiously Scots appellation "Auld Ridge" by the previous millionaire owner), stiff in his shiny rented tux, dwarfed by the portico's Ionic columns, his brother Johnny's jalopy defiling the wide, circular, sea-pebbled driveway behind him. Nancy's father was at work; this was soon after the divorce, after her mother had escaped to Manhattan. Were her sisters at home, giggling behind the bannister? Ushered inside, under a galaxy of a chandelier in the foyer, the family's Black butler Alfred must have helped Harry pin the corsage onto Nancy's gown.

That same evening my mother met my father's mother on the front stoop of the tidy O'Brien house in Arthur Manor, the wrong side of the tracks in Scarsdale. We were told this story countless times: my father opening the car door for my mother who tottered in her sister's heels up the slate walk toward his mother Gertrude, who held a Brownie camera in one hand, a Seagram's Seven in the other. Did Nancy curtsy in the porch light? She never mentioned many details, but she always landed the punchline:

"A pleasure to meet you, Mrs. O'Brien," my mother said. And Mrs. O'Brien mocked her to her face, parroting her sweetness, her country-club affectation: "A pleasure to meet you"— because already she knew who this girl was: "*Mrs. O'Brien.*"

Her House

MOST EVERYTHING WAS beige: the color of normal. The furniture was Ethan Allen or hand-me-downs of unmentioned provenance. Oil paintings hung here and there, gloomy garage-sale art depicting—not meaninglessly—boats tossed upon Turneresque seas.

The kitchen had some color: linoleum tiles a patchwork of faded moss green, tidal blue in the breakfast room, and a threshold saddle like driftwood between. Many tiles, cracked or missing, exposed the antediluvian tarpaper underflooring. Crumbs and dust and dirt washed up beneath an overhang of caramel-varnished cabinets affixed with tarnished, clacking brass pulls. A bottom, deep drawer wedged full of stained cookbooks, loose receipts, recipes ripped neatly from women's magazines, index cards typed with more recipes. A motley assortment of cutlery jangled when the cluttered top drawer was pulled open. In a corner cabinet a two-tiered Lazy Susan revolved wonkily to reveal stale cereal, damp saltines, dented cans of tuna and soup; then, revolving, still searching, again the same cereal, saltines, cans . . .

Then there was the range, with its greasy gas burners, white numerals smudged away from tacky knobs (black for stovetop, red for oven). We'd squint through pinholes in the encrusted range-beds to confirm that the life-preserving blue flame still burned. (Poor Joyce would check these pilot lights nightly, sometimes several times descending the stairs in her nightgown believing that she could smell our family's impending asphyxiation.) The stovetop's backsplash displayed the icon of a showman in tails and a chef's toque, the M and C vanished from the *AGIC HEF*. The embedded manual clock was correct twice a day.

The pantry closet was lined with curling contact paper and larded with flour, loose multicolored sprinkles, silver foil cupcake liners, baking soda and powder, instant hot cocoa packets, and dry dog food when the dogs were alive. An amber vial of vanilla extract. A broom, with its dustpan hung on a paint-swollen nail.

The Formica countertop was yellow with a metal ridge girding the edges. We'd wipe the surface clean with a damp cloth because Father disapproved of—because he was afraid of—the infectiousness of sponges. A window above the sink looked out across our backyard on a lonesome tree swing. Flanking the window were cabinets for flatware, drinking glasses that Father would blow into, then rinse at least twice (a habit we children adopted without thinking) before filling with water: "The best water in the country—from the Catskills," he would proclaim as if boasting. And almost always it was water he drank, now and then wine, and never liquor or beer, which made him sick to his stomach, he said, or milk, which a doctor had warned him against after a bout of kidney stones in his twenties.

The vinyl wallpaper, torn and blistered in places, depicted barnyard life, blocky and geometric: the farmer and his wife, cock and hen, horses and cows and sows repeating from the baseboard to the ceiling's cloudily discolored acoustic tiles.

The breakfast room was papered the same, and tattooed with scattershot stains of spaghetti sauce. We would eat—without

Father—at a small farm table with two benches, one long and one short, beside a radiator that hissed and knocked in winter behind its metal, confessional-style grille. A high chair was brought up from the basement when there was a baby, and placed beside a yellow-painted hutch junked with popcorn- and rice- and ice cream makers; on its open shelf we children would unwrap and arrange the oranges and grapefruits sent each Christmas without fail from somebody named "Nana Ruth," handwritten in block letters on the brown-papered parcel.

Mother complained often about a kitchen (though it seemed just fine to us) so cramped that our refrigerator had to live around the corner in the hallway by the back door. One day she would remodel, she would say but she never did—we couldn't afford it, was her explanation. So she remained stuck in the '70s, even the '50s, in the kitchen of a house her father had paid for in secret.

Of course I didn't know who had paid for the house; I don't know now. But how could a twenty-six-year-old man without gainful employment in 1970—at any time, really—have afforded a house in Scarsdale? Surely my mother's wealthy father disapproved of the marriage (they had eloped, after all) and bought this house for his daughter as insurance against his son-in-law's all-but-certain failure.

One rainy afternoon before cancer, when I was first researching a book about my family, having gone so far as to contact a few estranged relatives, stirring up the ghosts, I was attempting to meditate on an airplane as it descended into Heathrow. One of my wife's closest friends had just died of leukemia in a hospital in New Jersey on the eve of Hurricane Sandy. But otherwise things were falling into place. I felt lucky: my career was rewarding; people were publishing me, seeing my plays, flying me to London. My birth family had disowned me, but I was making sense of it, or trying to, with my writing. My wife sat beside me, five months pregnant with our daughter. And I found myself asking God or the universe or my subconscious—though I knew I should not—for a sign, some kind of proof that writing about my family was a morally defensible way to proceed, considering the emotional cost, to myself and others. I needed to know: was I on the right path?

We checked into a shabby-genteel hotel in Kensington. In the Shakespearean Suite my wife requested a better bed. As I hefted our bags the elevator doors juddered open to reveal, on the wall of the hallway in front of my face, a framed print of a painting I grew up with.

Ours had hung in our beige dining room, often hidden behind the swinging door to the breakfast room. But it was the same: the French artist Hubert Robert's 1775 *Ponte Salario*. Across a picturesque Roman pile of a toll bridge travelers drove their cows, tossing gold coins up to a veranda where an old woman in turn dropped more coins down like feathers. Ruddy-faced wenches in crimson skirts toiled in the arch beneath the bridge, filling jugs, scrubbing linens in this tributary of the Tiber. An unsavory type in a tricorn hat, sword on his hip, admired the women from across the water. A crone sat on stone steps enticing a cat toward her feet.

Surely this was the sign I had asked for. But what did it mean? Was it a blessing or a curse?

Hunger

OUR MOTHER SNEEZED in sunlight, stifled those sneezes in her dainty fist, often while religiously watching her midday soap operas. She chewed her lips nervously. With the laundry warm in the basket at her feet, she folded her children's clothes into ever taller, softly leaning piles, commentating upon who'd been murdered, who'd just awoken from their coma, whose twin had seduced whose wife, who was only now discovering his true parentage. We children would have to wait for a commercial break to ask, "Is there anything to eat?" Her shrug amounted to "Go see for yourself."

The reason we were hungry was that we were expensive, despite her envelopes stuffed with coupons. The empty brown paper grocery bags clogged the back hallway when she showed us the fresh receipts—at least two hundred a week! An unfathomable, unconscionable sum to us.

Breakfast, if we ate it, was dry cereal dusted with white sugar, or white bread toasted and spread with margarine. Mother slept in. If she was awake, she was busily preparing Father's breakfast-in-bed: orange juice from concentrate, half a salted grapefruit, shredded wheat with slices of banana and milk, toast with

Concord grape jelly (the only jelly for him), all carried upstairs on an oval Lucite tortoiseshell tray.

A good lunch at home was a hot dog slit then butterflied and fried. On bad days I made myself a sandwich of mustard and jelly. Our mother didn't eat lunch herself, maybe a bowl of Saltines. She didn't need food so why should we?

Oddly she wasn't thin, though not quite fat. "Let's see what *her* figure looks like after six children," she'd grumble about anybody's slender mother.

For school we made ourselves peanut butter sandwiches, packed them in brown paper bags that spotted with oil. By junior high I'd bring nothing and loiter, with the others from my neighborhood, where the cafeteria food line let out, begging the rich kids for spare change with which to buy microwaved French fries in Styrofoam cups. In high school I did without lunch altogether, eating nothing between breakfast and dinner through a day of classes followed by hours of sports, feeling for the first time the pride of the penitent.

Dinner might be mashed potatoes from a box, Stovetop Stuffing, Rice-A-Roni. London Broil, a rump roast, or a whole chicken on Sundays. From the Golden Horseshoe Shopping Center we'd order two plain pizzas, with Chinese food for Father on these nights: chicken-fried rice, General Tso's, or—ironically to me even then—a dish called Happy Family. There were deli meats for "make-your-own" dinners with a plastic container of rice pudding for her, a black-and-white cookie for Father. It seemed like every other night we ate patties of pan-fried ground chuck on an English muffin, a scoop of boiled-in-a-bag peas or green beans that only "husky" Steven could choke down, and an iceberg salad with tomatoes if Joyce was around to slice and dice. Paul kept his foods meticulously segregated on his plate, and only ate as much as he had to.

On Sunday mornings Mother would drive us downtown and send one of us inside with cash for a baker's dozen of warm bagels (mostly plain or sesame, a raisin-cinnamon for her). If she was in a good mood, she'd send us into the bakery too, for glazed doughnuts. We'd eat little else all day, the margarine and cream cheese and sugar sedating our brains as we bent uselessly, anxiously, to our weekend homework.

My second-grade teacher, a mighty miniature woman with hair like challah bread, often sent me home from school: I was too thin, too pale—surely I was sick. Mother would laugh it off and say simply that Mrs. Asner was obviously one of those hypochondriac types.

Sometimes I'd come home from school to find my mother talking on the phone in the kitchen. She never talked to friends—she didn't seem to have any. If the phone rang it was one of her sisters. Rarely it was Ilana, the wild one, married to her marine and living in New Hampshire. More reliably it was Gwendolyn, already matronly, whose husband worked for their father. Or it was the youngest sister, Darcy, who was in those days forever "trying to have a baby," whatever that meant. Once I hefted a new carton of milk to Mother at the kitchen table. She opened and poured. I drank; and gestured for another, and another, while she gabbed happily, inattentively pouring until the carton was empty. In the living room I hit the couch and slept until dark. She laughed whenever she told this story, as if tickled by my childish appetite.

Chores

WHEN WE WERE sick—and somebody was usually sick in a house with four, five, and eventually six children—we were quarantined. A lot of good that did. As a recovering hypochondriac I understand this compulsion to contain. Stay in bed, my mother was saying, keep your problems to yourself.

She would seem put out, or worse, if we needed help eating or drinking, or taking our medicine (pink amoxicillin, purple codeine). If we were lucky she'd let us lie on the couch with our blankets and pillows, a sleeve of Saltines and a glass of 7-Up. I watched Ronald Reagan's first inauguration on TV like this. And *The Price Is Right, Let's Make a Deal, Press Your Luck* ("No Whammies!"). But if Father caught us he would yell—something about slovenliness, but really it was his fear of germs again—and hurl our pillows up the stairs after our scurrying feet, our blankets trailing like rattails.

Once I had a fever and watched as Aunt Ilana, her husband and their two boys, entered the house by the front door beneath my bedside window. Then moments later they departed with my mother and father and siblings, all exiting in a line until the house was empty except for me, the sick one. I feel the same today as I did then, as I sit at my desk writing: this freedom of loneliness, for which I am mostly grateful.

I watched her unload the clean dishes, then load the dirty, securing myself beside her in a niche comprised of the dishwasher's door, dropped like a drawbridge, the cool tiled wall behind me, the sticky drawers to my right, and to my left the doorless doorway (in which our heights were etched incrementally) to the back hallway, where our inconvenient refrigerator hummed.

Or I sat in the detritus beneath the breakfast table with Chipper, stroking the sheen of his sleek brown paws. The best color in the world was brown, I informed my mother.

I helped her make the beds. Like gossiping maids we ballooned the sheets, fluffed pillows in place, flipped bedspreads up and over on the count of one, two, three. "You're my best helper, Danny," she said. Perhaps this was our first secret.

She threw her back out again. Or was about to—she could feel it. It was the new baby. How could we not sympathize? We did, and we didn't. It was our fault she felt this way; and it wasn't. It was a slipped or herniated disk (what was the difference again?) or nerves her torqued muscles had pinched. Her older sister Gwendolyn had recently undergone surgery; bad backs "ran in the family"—"so be careful," she could be counted on to advise us: "Lift with your legs."

She called us into the nursery (why was she in there? had she fallen?). The tangled branches outside the window seemed to mesh with her curly hair as she lay upon Sally's pillow, her legs splayed, her knees propped. She needed us to collect more pillows. She would not read or listen to the radio. She would endure as she deserved, with only the cobwebs and ceiling cracks for diversion.

And where was Father in all this? Working in the attic, as usual. We never saw him concerned for her health. He slid a piece of plywood between the mattress and the box spring on her side of the bed, for support.

Dr. Linden in Larchmont recommended a heating pad and warm baths. After the bath, her freckled skin moist and rosy, Mother would execute her vaguely yogic, confusingly erotic "exercises" on the beige wall-to-wall carpet in her room. On her hands and knees, reaching an arm ahead, toeing a leg behind, a towel beneath and a towel atop—until that towel slipped, which it always did, so she always finished naked.

Also on doctor's orders she would swim daily at the Scarsdale pool, and in the winter months indoors at the Jewish Y, in a bathing cap and a black one-piece, or in earlier days a floral skirted suit. Was I embarrassed for her? Or of her? I felt relieved watching her go and return refreshed, somebody new now, briefly younger for a spell, shaking the chlorine from her ears, pinching then huffing her nostrils, the long tendrils of her hair adhering to her neck, her suit straps biting into her soft shoulders.

I was six when she provisioned us with draw-stringed denim sacks, to fill with the dirty laundry we were now expected to wash and dry and fold ourselves. Soon we were doing the dishes—each of us had our own night or two. Mine was Sunday, the dreaded roast chicken dinner, when I'd plug my radio into a countertop socket and listen to Top 40 or a base-ball game, while scrubbing pots and pans for what felt like the entire evening.

She was forever asking us to go to the kitchen, go upstairs or downstairs, bring that something or other to her now please. And we'd comply—though not without recalling inwardly her streetwise father's retort to any and all inconvenient requests for help: "What's the matter, your arm broke?"

Saturday mornings were for "chores." She used that word so we did too, though friends found it archaic. ("What are you, a frontier family?") They were annoyed that I couldn't play outside with them until my chores were done, while they were allowed to sleep on weekends until noon if they wanted to.

We vacuumed, dusted, waxed our wood furniture. Windexed windows. The garbage, though, was mine alone: empty the kitchen daily, and any bin with diapers too; every bin in every room on Saturdays. I'd procrastinate. If Father detected the slightest odor he would bellow my name.

The back hallway was a purgatory of sooty green walls and finger paintings taped to high wainscoting, the dreariness interrupted only by the mudslide of the mudroom, an oversized closet junked with rubber boots (lined with bread bags for ease of insertion), warped wooden tennis rackets screwed lopsidedly into wooden presses, balls and bats and mitts and mittens with mitten-clips and orphaned gloves and recycled coats—the air in there frigid in winter, baking in summer; then out again into the hallway's tunnel and the back door's opaque windowpane.

Outside, atop vertiginous steps painted a bargain-priced maroon, I would survey my backyard kingdom: invisible cicadas rattling everywhere, crawling out of the earth and discarding their grotesque shells in the grass and weeds; a neighbor's cat creeping chin-deep in the pachysandra beneath leathery rhododendrons and the incarnadine, numinous azalea; our plastic swing meandering in the breeze beneath high hovering branches.

Then down the steps to reckon with our family's shame. For the raccoons would have raided our trash barrels again during the night, leaving scat like rotting cranberries and snarling clouds of flies in their wake. Once I scooped up white rice only to discover I was clutching a handful of wriggling maggots. I wore Father's work gloves after that. I held my breath until lightheadedness dazzled my vision, then breathed through my mouth as shallowly as I could manage.

One afternoon I lifted a lid to discover a raccoon inside. Hissing, it raised its hackles and bared its fangs and claws. I scrambled over the fence, careful not to spear a testicle on a splintery tine, as Father had said a cousin of his had done long ago, running from the raised shotgun of a girlfriend's irate father.

Mother wanted a cleaning lady like the other mothers had but Father wouldn't or couldn't pay. Cleaning the house was her job anyway, he said. And ours.

But somehow she prevailed. The cleaning lady arrived at our door one drizzly winter morning, having walked from the train or the bus from Yonkers or Mount Vernon or Washington Heights. In gray polyester, skirted and white-aproned. Light brown skin. Did she speak a word of English? Which war zone had she fled: El Salvador? Nicaragua? She came weekly, and we had to tidy up first, which confused us: What was the point then?

We were in school so we missed the drama. A link of the crystal chandelier in our dining room had disappeared, and Mother was sure that the cleaning lady had stolen it. Father had to fire her. Years later I found that missing link atop our china cabinet, furred with dust. Had our mother hidden it there? She said she needed help but the truth was she couldn't bear it.

I didn't resent my chores; I found I could almost enjoy them: washing and waxing the floors, pouring the Lysol into a bucket of scalding water, soaking and then wringing the rag. On my hands and knees reaching and wiping, shoving bucket-and-body back to reach and wipe again. With fingers and nails in the cloth, digging gunk out of corners and crevices, the soil-shadow of my hand materializing in the rag. Standing from my labor, leaping for the staircase to wait and watch the wetness evaporate in patches. Then, donning an old tube sock like a hand puppet, dolloping from the metal can until the cold wax soaked through, soothing the rough tiles smooth with their new shine. My hands steamed red and raw in the sun that streamed through the high glass panes in our front door.

The sweet chemical smell of cleanliness meant love. Because Saturday evenings, after chores, the house in order, Mother applied her tanning foundation, her blush and mascara, her coral lipstick, and she and Father would go out for dinner, returning home hours later relaxed, even affectionate, with a doggie bag from Manero's, the steakhouse in Greenwich where they'd first gone as teenagers, her breath and pores exuding gorgonzola and garlic and the spice of her Opium perfume.

Her Bedroom

THE BEDSPREAD WAS clover green and quilted with white thread in florets; in patches where the stitches were missing the fabric puffed slack. The headboard was mahogany with wide slats through which we might feel with our hands and bare feet the coolness of her red-and-blue floral wallpaper. The lamp on her night table was faux bronze, her touch-tone telephone was cream.

She slept on the side of the bed closest to the door, as she said any decent mother should. (One night in a cottage in the Adirondacks a crib collapsed, shooting baby Sally out bawling across the floor, and Mother leapt up and raced face-first into a misplaced wall.) I liked sitting on her bed alone. I liked to use this phone. Something of mine must have slipped between the mattress and her night table, and reaching into the crevice I encountered a graveyard of dry snot. So she picked her nose in bed and wiped it on the sheets—just like me! Though she was a grownup, and my mother.

She collected reading material bedside: Danielle Steele, Maeve Binchy, Mary Higgins Clark, or something literary by Anne Tyler or Annie Proulx. Scores of self-help books too, and magazines like *Redbook* and *Ladies' Home Journal.*

The two drawers in her night table contained intimacies beyond my comprehension, for example something that looked like a rubber yarmulke (a diaphragm, I would later ascertain) in a plastic clamshell case, zipped inside a fawn suede pouch like a penny purse. I was sitting in a Romantic poetry class in college a decade later when, seemingly apropos of nothing, I realized that the electric massager in her bottom drawer must have been a vibrator. She kept it snug beside a well-thumbed copy of *Dr. Spock's Baby and Child Care*, and Vaseline for taking our temperatures rectally (among other possible uses). Also her unfilled and unfulfilled diaries, yet more self-help books about marriage and mothering, a single sheet of notebook paper folded in fours on which she'd written in red ink: "After the miscarriage Harry wouldn't talk to me. As if I'm to blame! Thank God for Danny—at least he listens to me."

Her small desk faced the wall between two windows that looked out on our front yard, with its withered grass in winter, and across the street the overgrown empty lots we called the Swamp. Loose pencils and ballpoint pens, coins and bent paper clips, lick-and-stick stamps in rolls, and bills, and letters, and greeting cards for every occasion choked her desk drawers. Her blotter was a waxy green; the seat of her armless chair was green corduroy.

A rocking chair in the corner, richly stained, cushionless, curvaceous and imposing, was where she said she'd rocked us through our sickest nights as infants—an image of desperate loving care that I have always found incredible; that Father had rocked us too, as she also claimed, was inconceivable. I'd sit on the bed entertained by the feminine drama relayed by Joyce as she perched on the edge of this rocking chair, complaining to Mother about the girls who'd snubbed her at school, the boys who'd barked after her as she walked past them at the public pool. (Joyce took after my father's mother Gertrude, a martyr with a mean streak, my mother frequently confided in me, especially when the two of them had been fighting.) When I was older I'd sit in the rocking chair and listen to Mother as she lamented from her bed that her stepmother and sisters were disregarding her father's will, cheating her of her rightful inheritance, and I would pretend to understand the elaborate legal and moral reasons she gave for her grievance.

Her dresser was wide and low and mounted with twin tall mirrors, one tilted slightly for a lower view of the waist down. A top drawer was full of her underwear, the bras and panties I'd transfer when doing my laundry from washer to dryer in the basement, horrified by her stains.

I'd push on her door when the hook was in the eye on the other side, sunlight winking. "Go outside," she'd call skittishly, "to play!" They had sex punctually every Saturday morning; the torn condom wrapper in the bedroom waste basket it was my chore to empty would confirm this.

But why condoms anyway? Was her diaphragm deemed insufficient? Was she afraid the synthetic hormones in the birth control pill would give her breast cancer like her namesake, her father's mother Nancy? Did our father believe she was on the pill when sometimes, by design, she wasn't?

When I was a young man I sat eating lunch on a bench in a playground in midtown Manhattan with an actor I found attractive. We were on break from a play I had written, and she was acting in it. The actor's mother had died young of cancer; her father was a surgeon. When I mentioned that my parents had produced six kids, she remarked, "Well, they must've loved to fuck." The thought had never occurred to me.

One morning in high school after I'd fallen in love and had begun to fear the loss of it, I spied them through the hinge of their door, spooning in bed, eyes closed. He seemed to cling to her side, his arm thrown over the bowl of her hips, his nose in her hair.

One evening she wore a sweater only, her wide bush a blur. Her eyes locked with Father's across the bedroom as I walked in—and promptly spun around to flee. Father was fully dressed. It looked almost romantic, her humiliation.

Did they kiss in secret? I never saw them embrace. In Vermont at the inn across the lake from the camp where she'd been sent as a girl (against her will, she made clear)—the inn where even in the '70s waiters wore white shirts and black slacks and bow ties and vests; where we gorged ourselves on slabs of bacon, cakelike flapjacks sopping up the syrup as the mist rose off the lake, hot chocolate and warm cookies before bed; where we boys pulled our pajama pants into our cracks and danced around the cabin, provoking glorious spasms of laughter from her—I remember walking after dinner along the porch that lined the inn, mosquitoes biting and bats zigzagging and lake waves lapping, and while we children tromped ahead I looked behind and saw Father drape his blazer over Mother's shoulders and reach down to hold her hand. They may have kissed, though I doubt I would have forgotten the sight of something so rare.

I never felt closer to my mother than while lying in my bed on the other side of their bathroom wall. The rush of water through the pipes and the muted music of her voice as she talked to my father must have recalled the burble of conversation that filtered through the plumbing of her womb. And the sound of her bath in the afternoon calmed me: a sign of the day's contests postponed.

When I was afraid at night I would knot my fingers beneath my pillow and speak in my mind to God, but also to her, envisioning my thoughts traveling through the pipes of their bathroom and on, like electricity through the circuitry in the walls of their bedroom to her body and her brain, where she slumbered beside the ogre.

When they fought in their bedroom or bathroom she sounded subdued, stealthy (that genius IQ of hers again), as she goaded him into raising his voice, into outright shouting or punching the pale green tiles above their toilet. If I listened carefully with my ear to the wall, as I'd seen done on TV, words might slide into focus and I would learn—while the plug-in razor roved all over his round blandness, while he munched his chalky antacids—that he was angry at colleagues at work, in the days when he went out to work, or with a competitor or client who'd snubbed or wronged him. A flush midsentence meant one of them had been pissing or shitting in front of the other. I never understood how he could shout at his wife about things that weren't her fault, and how she could just sit there and take it.

There had to have been money problems. Bill Welsh, my mother's father, was the founder and president of a clothing corporation with three thousand employees, headquarters on the sixty-sixth floor of the Empire State Building, a retail hub in Louisiana, and overseas expansion in the '80s into thirty countries including Bangladesh, India, and South Korea. Rumor had it that he'd golfed with Nixon, which is probably why my grandfather was one of the first American businessmen authorized to recolonize China. My grandfather's company manufactured men's dress and business shirts for large retailers to sell as their own. Walmart was one of his clients, and the business was lucrative.

My mother had aspirations for my father to rise in the corporate world, but he always got fired (if he got hired in the first place). He attended the City University of New York for a semester or two, and after that acquired a certificate of some kind in the ascendant field of computer programming. He worked at PepsiCo in nearby Purchase, but they let him go; then at Sikorsky Aircraft just over the border in Connecticut until a fear of flying grounded that dream, as he found he was incapable of boarding a plane to attend far-flung meetings and conferences.

Wherever Harry found work he found he was disliked. So he'd dislike his coworkers and bosses in return, or dislike them preemptively from the start. He bought his *Playboy Party Jokes*—on its paperback cover a pen-and-ink minx wearing only evening gloves and thigh-high stockings, reclining invitingly in a bathtub-size martini—as a field guide to socializing around water coolers; to no avail. At my mother's urging he inquired about the possibility of working for my grandfather. His sister-in-law Gwendolyn's husband, Richard or "Dickie," was the company's heir apparent, and they lived in a rambling manse in Greenwich, replete with a striped marlin mounted on the wall of Dickie's oak-lined study. But my mother's father told Harry he wasn't hiring family anymore.

So Harry rented an office in the Harwood Building, a half-timbered, crenellated red-brick monstrosity in the mock Tudor style of Scarsdale's downtown, with twenty-two shops below and fifty offices above filled with doctors, dentists, lawyers. He hung out his own shingle: "Computer Consultant." My father would act the part of a suburban success until art could become reality.

But soon he was moving into a room in a shared office in Pound Ridge; then, soon again, up the stairs of our house he shouldered his desk into what had been the nursery. This was 1977. Before long he relocated, one last time, to an attic room—the room my brother would one day jump from—which he renovated with skylights, an air conditioner, and cozy wood paneling. Here, for the remainder of the century, he'd work—or pretend to work; his door stayed closed.

"I am the breadwinner of this family," our mother complained to Paul one morning at the breakfast table. Little by little she was forced to liquidate the company stocks that her father had given her in case of emergencies. "Your father," she told her oldest son, "hasn't worked in ages."

"It was vicious," Paul told me years later. "The way she talked about him. I felt bad—I mean for Dad. I don't know why she had to be so cruel."

Why She Had to Be

HER FATHER WAS an orphan, only eight years old the annus horribilis of 1921 when his parents died.

No wonder Bill Welsh worked obsessively. What other choice did he have? He hardly drank, wouldn't smoke (didn't trust it); he didn't have writing or Zoloft like I do. His business was his art, and his escape, and he proved to be an exceptionally accomplished escape artist.

My mother would invoke the tragedy of her grandmother Nancy's early demise whenever she reminded us of their shared name. She worried she would get breast cancer too; one of the reasons she'd had so many children, and breastfed us all, was because childbirth and breastfeeding was supposed to protect against the disease. There appears to be a link between breast and colon cancer; maybe the first Nancy's cancer-causing genes passed to me instead.

It was hard not to wonder about the facts of my grandfather's orphaning though, given our family's history of addiction and mental illness. What were the chances of both parents dying of natural causes in the same year? I dug up the death certificates for John and Nancy Welsh of Bayonne, New Jersey, and in both cases no cause was listed, as still happens today when a death might be regarded as shameful. Now I wonder less about "the chances," considering my wife's cancer and mine in the same year. Misfortunes, like fortunes of every kind, tend to compound.

Whatever the causes, his parents were gone, and my grandfather was carted off to live with his uncle Alex's family in the middle-class burg of Hempstead on Long Island; where one day Bill Welsh would meet the girl who must have reminded him of his lost mother, a sullen beauty he knew he could save with his success.

I don't know who my mother's mother Ruth was before her alcoholism, before her divorce and estrangement; or who she was after she moved to Florida, where she cohabitated with "Gigolo Joe" (at least that's what everybody called him because they never married, thereby ensuring my grandfather's ever-recurring alimony payments).

Ruth's maiden name was Anstey and she was proud of her direct descent from one Christopher Anstey, an eighteenth-century English poet laureate buried in Westminster Abbey.

Never mind that he'd never been poet laureate. And his grave is not in Westminster but in Bath, where he'd lived. But it is a fact that Christopher Anstey's name is inscribed on a white marble tablet in the south transept of Poet's Corner in Westminster Abbey, where it rubs shoulders with Shelley's. Some years ago a team of doddering black-robed docents took almost an hour to help me find him there.

Anstey is my sixth great-grandfather, if I'm counting correctly, and he's remembered (if remembered at all) for a best-selling book of satirical epistolary poems, written in anapestic tetrameter, concerning the arriviste Blunderhead family as they seek a cure in the Roman baths at Bath for a family-wide bout of chronic flatulence. He was forty-two when his masterpiece was published. I bought a copy in a used bookstore in Bath (they had a dozen or so, in as many editions). But allowing that satire is the most perishable of the literary arts, *The New Bath Chronicle*, dear reader, has not aged well.

I have seen displayed on the first floor of Beningbrough Hall in Yorkshire, home to several portraits on loan from London's National Portrait Gallery, a painting of Anstey by William Hoare of Bath, a framed print of which hangs above my desk in California today: the poet, middle-aged and gray-haired in a navy coat and waistcoat, ruffs at his cuffs and cravat, sits at his desk with his writing quill poised near the bottom of a page of foolscap. As if mid-thought, his expression is resolute, with just the slightest twitch of a Mona Lisa grin. He looks like me, I daresay, though his eyes are brown, as are his daughter's. Eight-year-old Mary Ann dawdles at his elbow, smiling impishly, one hand peeling back her father's lapel while the other shakes a champagne-pink "fashion doll" with "towering feathered headdress" ("clearly meant to recall Anstey's satire of such extremes of modern female fashion," reads the gallery catalogue's text). I adore this portrait because it reminds me of my dearest loves, my daughter and my work, and how truly there is no contest between them. At all times I welcome the distraction of my daughter.

My mother was like her mother proud of her Anstey lineage; she invoked it often as evidence that she and I had literature in our blood, and that at least her branch of the family was cultured and substantial. And this despite knowing very little about the Ansteys; I have only recently learned that Anstey's son John, my fifth great-grandfather, married Helen Senior, descended by a few centuries from Abraham Senior, court rabbi to Ferdinand and Isabella of Spain, who famously converted to Roman Catholicism in 1492 and then promptly expired. (Does that explain the curiously Sephardic hair my mother and I shared?) Some of Anstey's children and grandchildren were slaveholders in the West Indies, colonial bureaucrats in India, and committers of other atrocities. But by the 1930s our line of Ansteys had declined into a precarious middle class in Brooklyn.

My hard-drinking grandmother Ruth ended up living a long life, dying at ninety, just three months after I was married. My parents hadn't come to my wedding and we weren't talking. When my mother called I saw her number and didn't answer, so it was from a voice mail that I learned that Ruth was finally gone. She'd been wasting away in a nursing home on Cape Cod, cared for by my now divorced Aunt Ilana, the "wild" sister who alone had allied herself with their wild mother. I found it ironic, and insulting, that my mother would use the death of her estranged mother to try to manipulate me, yet again. I didn't return the call.

I was barely a teenager the only time Ruth and I met. Ilana had brokered an armistice. My mother was skeptical but she came along, without Father, to Darcy's house on the moneyed side of Long Island. (Darcy, after her hippie phase in college in Colorado, had sensibly married a Manhattan spice trader named Tad.) There were lots of grandchildren there. I strove all afternoon to impress my grandmother with my charm and maturity. I hoped she found me handsome. My mother was forever saying how I reminded her of her father; would I remind Ruth, too, of the man she'd fallen in love with long ago? She didn't look at me once that I recall. Neither did she look at my mother, or say much of anything, as she sat there in a lawn chair in the backyard. With her oversized sunglasses, her chin tilted imperiously toward the sun, her wrinkled hands motionless on her round lap, her body vacant: she was here and nowhere. I remember thinking that she looked the most like my mother, the daughter who hated her the most.

My mother almost never mentioned her early childhood in Garden City on Long Island. Where she loved school; where one day her teacher made a house call to inform my grand-mother that shy, secretive Nancy, the runt of the litter with hair like steel wool, was "a genius, as proved by the results of this IQ test." The teacher stood in the middle of the living room, clutching a paper with the numbers black on white. Ruth made this woman nervous, reclining there on the couch, sipping an early afternoon cocktail. "Your daughter ought to be skipped a grade," legend has the teacher saying, and Ruth simply laughed—scoffingly, cryptically. But Nancy did skip a grade; there was no denying her intelligence.

I don't have any photographs from my mother's childhood but I remember one: Bill and Ruth together in leafy sepia sun-light, at a garden party in Garden City perhaps, their gang of friends blurred along the edges. Bob's "bedroom eyes," as my mother called them (that bulged as he aged, like my mother's would, like mine are), his "Roman nose" (though he wasn't Italian) that I have inherited along with a broad, high forehead; he resembled in his early days a well-fed F. Scott Fitzgerald. In this picture he has curled his arm around his Zelda's shoulder, a blithesome Ruth with golden coif glowing, her head thrown back in laughter.

This may have been a photograph from before my mother was born, like her parents' wedding day, when Ruth was twenty and Bill was twenty-four. *The Long Island Daily Press*'s society page of July 1, 1935, describes a Lutheran ceremony attended by three hundred, followed by a reception for sixty at the bride's family's home in Bellerose. The paper's itemization of my grand-mother's apparel approaches, in my opinion, poetry:

> The bride, escorted to the altar by her father, wore a princess gown of ivory Chantilly lace. A tulle veil caught with orange blossoms fell from a small lace cap. Her bouquet was of lilies-of-the-valley and baby's breath.

The bridegroom is described as a student at New York University and an employee of the J.C. Penney Company, Manhattan. The newlyweds would honeymoon in the Adirondacks, then make their home in Jackson Heights.

When my mother's family became rich, after her father had gambled everything on a business of his own and made a killing, they would vacation in Jamaica in a jet set that included the actor Kirk Douglas, soon to be listed as one of Ruth's alleged lovers in the 1962 divorce proceedings. Another brush with fame in Jamaica involved Jack Kennedy: stung by a jelly-fish, my prepubescent mother came limping along the beach to the infirmary, where the junior senator from Massachusetts was just sitting there, in the flesh, waiting his turn. "He was so handsome," my mother would reminisce, though as far as I know she always voted Republican. "He'd been stung by a jellyfish too."

There's another photograph from her childhood that I can still conjure to mind: her older brother William Jr., or Billy, the firstborn, in a zip-up cable-knit on a beach (Long Island? the Caribbean?) gazing out at the waves beneath lowering clouds, spume and mist mixing above black rocks. She told us only that Billy had been "sent away" when he was twelve (she would have been five or six) because of a breakdown of some kind. She said it was autism, but she was protecting us, and herself, from the truth that her brother was a paranoid schizophrenic.

Society blamed mothers like hers; doctors in the 1950s called them "refrigerator mothers": cold, inhuman, malfunctioning women who reared dysfunctional children. She blamed this damning characterization for her mother's drinking. She blamed her mother too for what had happened to their family; she was confused: she couldn't blame her mother for Billy or she'd have to blame herself for my brother Paul.

Eventually Billy set Auld Ridge on fire—or tried to, anyway. No doubt he was simply hearing voices, doing what they told him to do, down in the heart of the house in the telephone closet beneath the grand staircase, let us speculate, with newspapers and gasoline, before Alfred the butler smelled smoke. Then fire engines lined that circular, sea-pebbled drive.

Bill Welsh paid a family of devout Christians in Calgary, Canada, to care for Billy, so he might live near a doctor famous—and ultimately infamous—for claiming to cure schizophrenics with massive doses of niacin. Billy, of course, remained schizophrenic. Maybe my mother's resistance to psychotherapy wasn't simply denial, but braided with the bitterness of her brother's failed treatment? I have no proof that he was lobotomized, but historically the timing was right. My mother never saw her brother again—I don't think any of her family did, except Ruth, who made a point after the divorce of visiting her son Billy in Calgary on holidays and birthdays.

On my birthday the phone might ring. "Danny?" she would say if I answered, "this is your Nana Ruth," though we hadn't met yet. She sounded like my mother: the same eerie, vacant chattiness. "You and I were both born on the same day. Did you know that? And *my* mother too."

Then she'd put Uncle Billy on: "Hi," he'd say dopily, like a kid. "Do you like baseball?" and I'd have to admit that yes I did like baseball and hoped to play professionally one day, but by then Billy would have hung up.

Mother and I laughed one day at a snapshot she'd been sent of Ruth and Billy wearing conical birthday hats, elastic straps pouching their saggy cheeks and chins. Flaccid balloons lolled along the sunny kitchen table in Calgary where they sat. In this picture Billy had the look of an institutionalized lifer, at once his age and ageless. When my grandfather died, the obituary in the *New York Times* didn't include Billy's name.

After their parents' divorce, I imagine my mother and her sisters in a four-seater on the commuter train to Grand Central, looking prim and grim. Then walking forlorn down toward the East River into, let us say, Murray Hill (I've never been able to learn where precisely Nana Ruth lived, for a time, in Manhattan); or crawling through inclement weather in a cab. Then the bravest of them climbing the steep brownstone steps to press their mother's cracked buzzer . . .

Nancy and Ilana were teenagers by this time. Gwendolyn was already married and pregnant with the first of her five children. Then Darcy, the youngest, as towheaded and guileless as she'd remain, or try to remain, evermore.

The windows in my grandmother's postdivorce apartment in Manhattan were grimy with soot, my mother told us. Every visit the girls would fill a bucket and scrub the windows clean, squeezing the gray water from the rags and dumping the black down the drain.

My grandfather ended up owning vacation homes in Vermont and Florida. Most of the time he lived with his second wife, Regina, a handsome, brassy career woman a dozen years younger than him, in a high-fenced midcentury ranch in

Harrison with his faithful butler Alfred, now grown old, and two frothy Doberman pinschers; then later in a luxury condominium at the Westchester Country Club in Rye. Both homes were just a short drive from our house in Scarsdale, yet we'd see Bill and Regina only on a Christmas or Thanksgiving afternoon, for an hour or two. My grandfather had adopted Regina's son Jason, who lived with them through college in his own suite like a bachelor pad, with leopard-print sheets on a king-size waterbed. My grandfather bought Jason a black Trans-Am with vanity plates that read, rather menacingly, "JAW"—his new monogram—and when Jason totaled it and survived unscathed, my grandfather wrote the president of Pontiac a fan letter extolling the sports car's laudable safety features.

In his older age Bill Welsh looked like a trimmer J. Edgar Hoover, almost always standing, jangling a bunch of loose coins in the deep pockets of his slacks, declaiming about anything in his gruff New Yorker's bark. Or businesslike he'd shake our soft hands with the claw he'd developed, his pinkie and ring finger curled tightly into his palm (a condition called Dupuytren's contracture, or "the Celtic hand," inherited no doubt from his Scottish ancestors). He liked to tease me by calling me "Joe Hardy" because when I was three or four years old I'd wanted to try on the name of the handsomer of the two Hardy Boys, boy detectives. "How ya doin', Joe Hardy? Give me some skin, Joe Hardy!" he'd say as he bent, knees popping, back stiff, so I could slap his liver-spotted claw. When I was a teen I might answer the phone to his falsetto voice saying "Hello? Is Joe Hardy there? This is his girlfriend Mabel"—or Gladys or Agnes or Ethel, the damsels of his Depression-era youth.

When my mother had babies, her father didn't visit her at the hospital, but only telephoned. She'd pull herself up in bed, exposing her curiously deflated belly, to receive his brisk well-wishes. Yet my mother worshipped her father and would retell these quasi-mythical anecdotes about him all the time. Like the Christmas Eve when they'd gone to bed without a tree or gifts; as usual their father was working late in the city, their mother was drunk, but after midnight the children awoke to the tremor and exhaust of a cargo truck, their father in the driveway directing the deliverymen as they unloaded a pre-decorated tree and a bonanza of gift-wrapped goods.

Something she never talked about, though, was what his workaholism revealed: an all-consuming fear of penury that was really a fear of helplessness—of losing his parents again, as if that were possible. His compulsion to provide for his family was, paradoxically, what destroyed his family, at least in part. He cheated, I'm sure, in business and probably in love. He evaded the military in World War II (purposefully or not, I'll never know) by consistently having children; just as the rules changed, he and Ruth would produce another. He must have worried—like I do—about everything. Those coins, again, jingling in his pocket. The cheese nibbled and milk sipped nightly for his ulcer. His fear of heights, despite or because of his company headquarters in the Empire State Building, a vulnerability he coped with every morning by pulling the shades in his office all the way down.

But could it have been worse? My mother hoarded and nurtured her secrets; behind every pitiable reminiscence she shared there lurked something unspeakable, an unforgiveable injury that had wormed itself into the heart of her: "You'll never know how bad it was for me . . ." Then shaking her head gravely, wistfully even, drifting out of reach again . . . She would write a memoir of her childhood troubles, she often confided in me, if only she could find the time. But even then I knew that what was stopping my mother from telling her story was not time but fear.

Since I was an adolescent I have suspected that my mother was sexually abused as a child. I felt it in my bones, in my blood, in my own body, if such a thing were possible. I have no proof. But did her schizophrenic brother molest her before he was sent away? Was that *why* he was sent away? Was "setting the mansion on fire" a metaphor for what he had done to her? Did he stand outside her bedroom door naked, babbling about God? Did he wake her in the night with his touch?

Was it her father? I was like him, she told me often, in my appearance and demeanor, and there's no doubt she committed a kind of emotional incest with me. She spoke about her father with an erotic intensity. He would take care of her until his death and beyond—secretively, financially—in dribs and drabs like he was the victim of long-term extortion.

Or he was indebted to her for a different reason. As I grew older, as I learned to accept her weakness for deceit, I've wondered if my mother concocted the story that led to her father winning custody—or embellished it, at least. The official story, one my mother told from time to time, was that Ruth had been drunk again one afternoon at Auld Ridge, wearing a mink (a full-length? a stole?) over only her bra and panties, intent on traipsing across their vast undulating lawn toward a neighbor's house to borrow some vodka, the way other mothers borrowed butter or flour. She was barefoot, or wearing high heels. My mother was perfectly aware, at the age of twelve, that their neighbor was providing more than alcohol.

My mother blocked the door. Ruth hit her, kicking and scratching, shouting and spitting until, worn out, she lost consciousness on a couch. My mother fell asleep on the floor in front of the door, thus ensuring that when her father came home from work and found her, bruised and bloodied, he would finally have the evidence he needed to divorce his wife and keep custody of his daughters—"his girls," as he called them.

Maybe, after all, her mother's physical abuse was the worst of the trauma she suffered, and the rooted depths and branching reach of this pain was the bodily shame I sensed in her. Taking her story at face value, it's understandable that she and my grandfather shared an intense bond, and a peculiar guilt.

And still the mystery remains. "He wasn't perfect either," my mother said to me that February morning in 1995, in the crowded cathedral in White Plains, as she turned away from her father's purple-palled casket. Her bloodshot eyes were wet not with grief but rage: "He did things he should have been ashamed of." But this was a story she never told.

Autobiography & Memoir

WE WERE THE reason why she didn't write, but she never said so. She'd say, rather, that her ambition to be a mother was greater than her ambition to be a writer. Or to invert a cliché of the writing life: her children were her books, each child a gift from the muse, our composition and reception in the world a mystery to her (though I was her best seller, so to speak, or so she expected of me). Still, she could grow melancholy when the subject of her literary aspirations came up.

"Why don't you just do it?" I'd say, especially when she was ruminating aloud, again, about her childhood. "Just write it. Write it all down. You don't have to publish it." But she would only smile weakly and shake her head.

I still think she could have done it. She was smart, maybe truly a latent genius of some kind. I understood her manifold unhappiness as a warning of the dangers of an ambition unheeded; instead of making art, her mind spent its considerable powers weaving her obsessions and delusions into intricate tapestries with which to deceive herself and her children. Telling and retelling her version of our family tragedy became the Gothic masterpiece that she could never bring herself to set down in words.

But she loved books, and I'm thankful for that. Nightly at the breakfast table where we ate our dinner (without Father; in those days he chose to eat by himself in front of the TV in the living room), breathlessly she would regale us with recaps of the latest chapter she was reading. John Irving was a long-ish phase; the weirdness of his families fascinated and tickled her. When I was older and starting to write short stories, she told me—with unmistakable ambivalence—that my writing reminded her of Irving's. "You will write about me one day," she'd say, as if prophesying her own death, "I know it." And yet how could I not? My whole young life she was filling me with her stories.

Once in a while she'd get the itch, or summon the courage, to enroll in a continued ed course. Am Lit & Civ was her passion. "That's what I'd study if I were your age," she'd tell us, weekly stealing away to Purchase College or Manhattanville College, leaving the older kids to look after the rest. Afternoons faded into evenings before she'd come home laden with armloads of paperbacks, dog-eared and underlined, highlighted yellow, orange, blue, dispensing anecdotes about her imbecilic, provocative, gifted classmates. The essays she typed on the Smith Corona in the attic came back to her invariably marked with As and A-pluses.

Her favorite course was by far autobiography and memoir, from John Muir to Annie Dillard, from *The Narrative of Sojourner Truth* to *I Know Why the Caged Bird Sings*. She found tales of subjugation inspiring. But these classes were fits that passed.

Similarly she'd withdraw as if chastened from her sporadic forays into the workplace. She wanted to write for the *Scarsdale Inquirer* but they never hired her. She volunteered for schools and churches, editing newsletters and issuing press releases. But she wasn't taken seriously, she complained, without a degree and with six kids. And in the end Father put his foot down. He—and we—needed her at home, she said.

Aunt Gwendolyn told me that my mother considered herself lucky. And it's true, my parents had been spared most middle-aged calamities: divorce, bankruptcy, cancer. I was interviewing Gwendolyn on the phone for this book; elderly Uncle Dickie was shoveling the snow from their driveway in Greenwich. She kept herself understandably aloof, but nevertheless she talked. She had questions for me too. It had been more than twenty years.

I was flabbergasted—"lucky"? My mother had talked endlessly of her misfortunes, her neglect and abuse at the hands of those who should have loved her, and she'd diligently performed her misery for her children.

But sometimes I think I understand. Her son had tried to kill himself; perhaps she'd been wise to abnegate her life, to retract from joy—if she'd ever reached toward it—so as to subsist as safely as she could. Whenever I have felt a failure in my career, my marriage, my health, I have heard my mother saying, *See? You should have lived like me. You should have loved nothing and nobody, not even yourself.*

On the other hand, as Gwendolyn elaborated: "I just don't think your mother's had an easy life . . ." When I pressed her why—what, in her opinion, had been so difficult for my mother?—she answered with a question of her own: "What was the matter with your father? Have you figured that one out yet?"

II. His Failure

Orpheus

THE STORY GOES: she was riding the subway, a wintry dusk, sun setting behind skyscrapers, rosy clouds above and behind the brutal man-made canyon. Where my mother was coming from or going to I don't know; she was noticeably pregnant with their first child, Joyce—when the lights went out across the city. Flickering flames from cigarette lighters illuminated their faces; a businessman offered his seat. Everybody was polite, Mother would say: "It was a different time." Hours passed, snacks were shared. A policeman materialized in the tunnel and pried open a door with a crowbar and marched them out along the tracks, rats squealing in the subterranean murk. Father had driven down from their apartment in Tarrytown, trawling from street to street until he saw his young wife pulled through a manhole into a Times Square lit by head- and taillights; the gaping searchlight of a full moon, civilians conducting traffic. A National Guardsman, rifle slung across his back, held Mother's elbow as he handed her off to Father. Then into the car and back north again to Westchester he bundled her as if he'd saved her, and his unborn family, from the abyss.

Let It All Out

HE SAT IN a rowboat with friends shooting the rats that skittered beneath the docks in Pearl River, New York. Or were they floating on Uncle Marv's lake in Sullivan County? Or there were no friends—I'd never known my father to have any, just brothers or cousins. But he was happy there with the sun on the water, blasting rats to bits of blood and fur. He told this story to his children often and with relish, as if joking.

He cleaned his rifle sitting on his side of the bed, the door left wide. I can still smell the oil, hear the slide and chink of the bolt. Sunlight shone in the luster of the polished wood stock and in the ebony of the barrel.

Soon after his son's suicide attempt, Father took Paul to a gun shop and bought him a .22 of his own, then to a gun range to shoot; as if trying to make a man of his inadequate son, as if daring him to try to kill himself again.

Not long ago I tracked down my father's younger brother Brian—the lost one, the screwup, the hippie and rumored criminal—and he described my father as "a psychopath." Harry's innate insensitivity. His small unreadable eyes.

He hit us only a few times, when we were too young to hit

back but old enough to have said something true.

As soon as he entered a room we would feel compelled to leave, muttering "I've got homework to do . . ." Or without speaking we'd pay the powder room a pointless visit, or slip upstairs, or outside to play. We hoped to protect his feelings, but ours too; if he knew how we felt about him then our fragile sense of safety would be that much more endangered. When he was sitting there in the living room already, where he watched TV every night for hours, we stayed away. A normal man would have been hurt.

He gave the kitchen a prison-style shakedown. He disapproved of Mother's cooking and housekeeping, and some nights he cracked: pots and pans and bowls and plates and glasses and cutlery, all clattering to—some shattering off—countertops and floor. The dogs whimpered and cowered as Mother hustled the children upstairs.

We went to Friendly's for dinner, a frugal choice for our growing brood. Hot dogs staining the buns orange. Fribbles. We piled into the pleather booth. "You're in for a nice surprise!" was the slogan. Until one night he felt slighted—something that made no sense to us. The hostess kept us waiting, or sat us near the toilets; the waiter was too slow, too stoned. Our father lost his temper and threw us back into the car.

In Lake Placid, his preferred retreat from the humidity and pollen of August, they couldn't find our reservation. He ranted until he hyperventilated, his face swollen like a blood blister. We waited, watching, anticipating a heart attack with mixed feelings. But his anger won: we would have our adjoining rooms.

We drove to the top of Whiteface Mountain for the panoramic view. The Olympics had blown through town the year before, and souvenirs were heavily discounted. He bought me a patch depicting the mountain, for Mother to sew onto the breast of my Yankees jacket.

Late in the afternoon we sat in our station wagon, beige and wire-wheeled with wood siding, in the Holiday Inn's parking lot, watching the lightning flash over the mirror of the lake below. Thunder, a deluge of rain until our windshield was roaring as if with rage, and release.

When he drove us anywhere, which was rare, he would crane his neck and grit his teeth while looking behind and reversing down the driveway, his arm thrown back over the front seat toward our faces and we'd flinch. Never closer to our fear; the meaty hairy arm of an imponderable threat.

Did he ever tell a joke that wasn't an insult? And still we laughed, together, often, at what we as a family found absurd or annoying, pathetic or sad, about others. Turning off Post Road and down Grand Boulevard past his alma mater IHM (Immaculate Heart of Mary), he'd quip "Institute for Helpless Morons," and we'd laugh at—even take pride in—his brazen apostasy.

He liked to make fun of people who were having fun: playing their music loudly on the beach, in their car with the windows down; laughing too loudly, or dancing. "Idiots," he'd say, an almost involuntary epithet from him for just about everybody.

When wet snow toppled a tree in the Peerys' front yard, crumpling the hood of their Datsun, he turned out the lights inside so that we might better watch unseen at our windows, laughing as lights blinked on in their house and the Peerys dribbled out into the storm to assess their loss.

Or he could be in a good mood, shockingly. Sunday evening and he and Mother were drinking Blue Nun; some slight victory in business, perhaps. Regaling us from the head of the table in the dining room with tales of his boyhood, and one poor boy in particular whom he and his gang liked to pick on. Andrew was his name, but everybody called him Doo-Doo in imitation of his Polish mother who, summoning her son home for dinner, would call from their front stoop, high-pitched and melodic, "Doo-Doo! Doo-Doo!"

One day the gang convinced Doo-Doo he could fly. Superman was on TV. He tied a bath towel around his neck like a cape and climbed onto the roof of his family's garage. The gang cheered. He leapt headlong, fists thrust forth, and shattered both legs. Years later, his older brother threw open the car door and pushed Doo-Doo tumbling into traffic. Another time, the gang lured him into a wigwam of sticks and set the sticks ablaze; he raced from the inferno screaming, hair and eyebrows and lashes singed. Doo-Doo suffered a nervous breakdown in his twenties, Father told us without a hint of remorse. What an idiot. We all laughed until we cried.

It occurs to me that Doo-Doo was my father. It can't be true. There was too much sadistic joy in these stories. But my parents gave their children the most boring names they could imagine; less liable to be twisted into teases, they explained. Maybe my father was who he was because he was Harold, or Harry, or some mocking nickname, and he was bullied like Doo-Doo. I'll never know.

My father said that his father died of a heart attack at only sixty-two because his whole life he had "held it all in," meaning his emotions. My mother never said anything about her father-in-law except that he was "very nice," but she'd say it with an arched eyebrow, a pitying shake of her head, implying that it was the niceness that killed him.

For the sake of his health my father was determined to "let it all out," not unlike a downpouring thunderstorm in Lake Placid. Though by "it" he didn't mean every emotion (assuming he was capable of the full spectrum)—just displeasure, derision, vituperative rage. He would not live and die like his father, a career failure or at best a disappointment; and a henpecked husband too, one assumes, as such a large portion of my father's anger was reserved for his wife, and the six children he begrudged for receiving the love that should have remained his.

Neighbors and relatives were "puppy kickers," he'd say. But it was our father we saw kicking our dogs, and first when they were puppies.

Chipper was adopted roadside in Dutchess County. There must have been some collie in Chipper, because when he wasn't lethargic he was attempting to herd his own fanning tail in a dervishing blur. He'd fail, then fall, then under the table he'd slink again. The vet diagnosed him as depressed and suggested a companion, so our parents bought a puppy-mill cocker spaniel they named Mikey, who cheerfully set about dominating Chipper, often sitting for hours upon our morose mutt's long dry snout.

They ran away every chance they got—snaking around a closing door, yanking free of a leash. I didn't blame them. I assumed all dogs longed to escape their masters.

Often they were bad, wolfing a whole chicken off the platter on the countertop, or pissing on the living room's already piss-stained rug. Their yelps rebounded off the resounding kicks my father delivered to their rib cages and rumps, as they scrabbled down the stairs to the basement in the dark.

I came home from school one afternoon to find puddles of blood all over the kitchen floor. From their mouths and rectums. Something was wrong with our dogs—a virus, Mother told us. They disappeared.

Father had seemed to hate their wild helplessness; it was a lesson we children took to heart.

Fixing the house was constant. We boy-children would have to shadow him, veering inwardly between oppressive boredom and the panic of rookie wartime nurses, hustling downstairs to his basement workbench to fetch him a tool and all too often returning empty-handed, breathless, shamefaced. Simply the fear of not finding what he'd requested could render these items invisible. With his black horn-rimmed glasses fogged and crooked, his dyspeptic hiccupping and farting ("Who stepped on a duck?"—"Hey, another loose floorboard!"), with his comb-over wilting in strands atop a purpling, perspiring forehead, veins protruding, pulsating, we were forever expecting that half-hoped-for heart attack.

And woe betide our mother if ever she tried to involve herself in this masculine work—Father dismissed her with disgust.

And all the while he swore: "shit," "piss," peppered with a "fuck" in the noncopulatory sense; never a "cock" or "cunt" that I recall. Excrement was my father's métier. On one occasion we heard him say the word "condom," "pubic" another time, and he sounded so prudish, disgusted, his consonants cutting, vowels clipped, as if stabbing at the mere notion of sex with a litter stick.

I learned early that I could be foul-mouthed too. I was walking a girl home from school. She was an O'Brien like me, which unnerved me because I liked her, and I hoped to impress her with my worldly command of the profane. I forget the word I used, but she rebuked me—"My family doesn't speak like that," accelerating in her mincing step downhill toward her, no doubt, immaculate home.

So we were a dirty family then, sordid even. Within reason: we weren't allowed to curse at our parents, or at each other (at least not in our parents' presence). But the dirty world at large was deserving.

My father had apprenticed with his father, long enough to see what plumbers dealt with: "One day I just woke up and realized," he often told his children, as if imparting some great wisdom, "that I didn't want to spend the rest of my life up to my neck in other people's shit."

Though he ended up rejecting the family vocation, he remained handy and kept the house in order—or we did, as his labor crew. As a child I worried that all the varnish, turpentine, and bleach we used at his direction—most weekends, each and every school break—might give us cancer. We didn't don rubber gloves, or paper masks while scraping and sanding. We'd bump our heads against flaking asbestos-wrapped pipes in the basement, and filaments would drift through the air before our eyes. He'd assure us there was nothing to worry about, and leave us alone to finish the work that he had begun.

I must admit I am useless today as a man around the house. I acquired none of the workmanlike skills my father ought to have taught me, or I ought to have learned. When I build or repair, even artistically, I sense my father's sneer: *Of course you'll fuck things up. Idiot.*

He called it his bureau and kept it shut. If I stood on their bed I could scan the top:

An airbrushed glamour shot of our mother when she was young, with her anthracite eyes and belligerent jaw, set in a gilded frame, the overall effect both pretty and chilling.

His military-style paddle brush, with its blond wooden base and bristles soft enough to spare his thinning hair. (He'd palm it gently as he glossed his graying fringe.)

A flat wooden caddy to receive the mixed silt of spare

change and lost buttons, loose bills and lip balm and receipts
and God knows what else.

The laminated prayer card from his father's funeral.

The pewter Saint Christopher's medallion that was also a
pillbox, embossed with an image of the avuncular martyr carrying the child Christ on his shoulders across a river in relief.
Flipping it open with my thumb, I found inside not pills but
heavenly white wads of cotton.

Christopher is the patron saint of travelers, among others;
did my father use this medallion as a charm against his flying
phobia? Were those cotton wads for cushioning the Valium
tablets I discovered in an orange pharmacy bottle in the bottom drawer of his night table? Or was his Saint Christopher
meant to ward off death in general? Like that which took his
father in the middle of the night: "A dark time," Mother would
say darkly of the year before I was born.

Swinging wide the saloon doors of his bureau I'd slide the
drawers open into sunlight, dust rising like steam. His con-
servative attire folded neatly inside—slacks and collared shirts
and cardigans—seemed to have survived another century, a
forgotten country, a lost war. And I would wonder where he'd
come from. I had next to no idea.

Where He Came From

His small eyes were mole-like, sunk behind thick lenses in those thick black frames. The rare glimpses we had of him without his glasses, in bed on a Father's Day morning, he'd look helpless, squinting his dark blue dots at the gift-wrapped offerings jumbled upon his blanketed, undersized feet.

He was born too soon and the nuns assumed he'd die. His mother was unconscious from the anesthesia, so in the hospital sink they christened him "Patrick"—a safe bet for yet another Irish Catholic in the world. When his mother revived and held him to her breast, kicking and colicky, she rejected this stupid bog-hopping cliché of a name. She rechristened him Harold, which she found princely, upwardly Anglo, and the name of a much-loved deceased farmyard horse of hers to boot. But everybody would call him Harry.

For some reason he retained Patrick as his middle name and passed it along as a middle name to his firstborn son, Paul, the son most like him: those same small eyes, the same trouble with strangers and friends, though Paul could be kind.

My father's premature birth was blamed for the size of his eyes, as if this aspect of his anatomy had failed to develop fully during his truncated term in the womb. Mother liked to describe his eyes as "deep-set," as if deep inside his expression-less face his eyes were in fact normal, just as somewhere deep inside his psyche (his children could be forgiven for hoping) our father loved us. But it made sense to us that he'd been born with some sort of congenital deficiency, for in those instants when we could not help but make eye contact with him, we saw: his eyes went nowhere.

As with his eyes, so too his lineage. I know precious little about the O'Briens. My father didn't speak of them except to per-petuate the myth of five O'Brien brothers fleeing the Famine and tumbling onto the docks in Manhattan, where they traded their rags for Union uniforms, a hot meal, a rifle, and a train ticket south. Where four of the five were promptly slaughtered on the battlefields of Maryland or Virginia or Tennessee.

His father, John Edward O'Brien, was born in Fordham in 1909. My uncle Brian painted a fanciful picture for me of these Bronx O'Briens as "rum runners and gun runners, gangsters, priests, nuns. Real mean sons of bitches. Full of envy—just like your father."

Their mother Gertrude was born in 1915 in Suffern Rock, Rockland County, New York (two "rocks" in the details of the birth of a woman who, by many accounts, could be hard and cold). Seven years earlier her father, James "Pop" Colwell, had shipped from County Cavan via Londonderry on the SS *California* into Ellis Island.

Pop, or Jim or Jimmy as he must have been known as a young man, stayed first with his sister Bridget, where she lived as a servant at 5 Bank Street in Greenwich Village, the same five-story brownstone where Willa Cather was living and writ-ing some of her most celebrated work. (I don't know if Bridget actually worked for Cather—my father never mentioned it;

but then again he'd probably never heard of Willa Cather.) Through the 1920s Jim was a gardener, tending the grounds of St. Michael's Home for Children, a Catholic orphanage on Staten Island. But when the Depression hit he was a farmer an hour north in Spring Valley, just over the border from New Jersey, though what he farmed is anybody's guess. All we children ever heard about Pop Colwell was that he smoked cigars and drowned puppies in sacks with bricks.

My uncle Brian sent me a photo album recently, like a book of spells with parchmenty pages and a scaly crimson cloth cover, full of photographs of his mother's life when she was no longer a girl but not yet their mother. On a sheet of legal-size paper, in large neat penmanship, Brian wrote: "You of all people deserve this."

The photos are black and white, of course, faded to sepia, tucked into black-tabbed corners (where corners remain) or secured with bits of brittle tape; or loose, fluttering free when I crack the binding. Their borders and backsides are annotated with the inside jokes and slang of a forgotten epoch: "Nerts" and "Schmokin'" and "Looking flash!" There's nary an indoor shot in the collection, as if it had been summertime always in Rockland during the Depression. Teenage boys sport dapper haircuts and high-waisted pants, or they're laughing in sundresses—crossdressing for a lark, one presumes; or they stand long-legged in a row in woolen bathing suits like singlets. Spots of sun damage float above the faces of hulking nuns, glowering in the borders of these festive photographs like referees, or inquisitors. The girls look sweet, fetchingly posed in skirts against a rock wall, or in their high school graduation caps and gowns like a grinning Gertie in a snapshot marked '33.

In another photo Pop stands atop a ladder, wiping a windowpane, neat in his gingham shirt and overalls. With his polished-bald head and his broad cauliflower nose, a corncob pipe (what about those cigars?) clamped tight in a lantern jaw, he looks a lot like my father.

Next, the Colwells pose proudly in front of their black Model T, Pop and his five children in descending birth order: Bill, Gertie, Mary, Alice, Anne, and Jimmy. They were "insulated for the most part from the Depression," Brian wrote to me. "Pop was a man of standing—a good family, though the girls' moral character was often in question. Swimming, movie mags, books, football, skating, waiting for the next adventure. They never saw the war coming. Bill was sent to Europe, where he was one of Patton's photographers and helped record for history the liberation of the concentration camps. Jimmy went to the Philippines where he was a prisoner of war and, though he came home, he never recovered. Anne's husband was shot down and killed. Their lives changed overnight and forever."

But these are photos of life before the war, before marriage and parenthood for my O'Brien grandparents; these images record, however impressionistically, that summer idyll when Gertie met Johnny as he convalesced at a nearby rest home from a rheumatic fever, brought on by scarlet fever, that had scarred his heart. In the '30s young Johnny would play in the New York Yankees farm system, or so the family said, but this heart condition kept him from climbing the rungs into the big leagues. His health kept him from active duty in the war too. He'd spend those years at the Brooklyn Navy Yard, developing "intricate top-secret bomb sights and fusing mechanisms for ships," according to Brian. "So much for the dumb-ass plumber!"

My grandfather in his sleeveless undershirt smolders in these Depression-era photos like a young Marlon Brando, or smiles, natty in necktie and suspenders, displaying the gapped front teeth my father would inherit, as he poses in the grass with his sweetheart Gertie by his side. They're holding hands—all four hands, in fact; she looks sad yet sweetly so, demure in her floppy bobby socks. Gertie's mother died young—of what, I do not know—and it fell to her as the oldest girl to raise the rest. She never had a childhood of her own. "By the time she got married she was sick of being a mother," Uncle Brian spelled it out for me. "But she made the mistake of having us anyway."

Like most O'Briens in those days my grandfather was a laborer. He worked from home, and ran this ad regularly in the *Scarsdale Inquirer*: "John E. O'Brien, Plumbing & Heating, 167 Madison Road. Alterations, Repairs, New Work." His phone number like everybody's was four digits.

At a professional peak in the '50s he opened a plumbing supply store on Scarsdale Avenue, close to the train station and the barbershop, but it didn't last. Gertrude had to work as a cashier nearby just to make ends meet. My father and his brothers were outclassed in Scarsdale. Their father was fixing the toilets of the rich, like celebrity jeweler Harry Winston. Murderer Robert Durst, son and heir to real estate mogul Seymour Durst, who'd watched his mother leap to her death from the roof of their estate around the corner from Scarsdale High, was a classmate of my father's, as was Liza Minnelli, who starred in the school drama club's *Diary of Anne Frank* before touring the production to Israel. Harry must have felt inferior, at best ill-equipped; but one day, with the help of my mother—and my mother's family's money—he would escape who he was.

After John O'Brien died of that heart attack, when my father was twenty-seven, Gertrude started drinking heavily. Hung over one morning, she broke her ankle stumbling out of bed. She moved to Miami, where she purchased a set of large kitchen knives to protect against a home invasion by the Cuban "boat people," she said.

A Hollywood psychic, though he lives in Burbank and grew up in Appalachia (his persona is delightfully hillbilly-Liberace), once instructed me to list the names and birth dates of the departed loved ones I wished to contact. I handed the paper back to him. When his finger reached *Gertrude* he gasped theatrically: "Lordy! Did you ever see your grandma's hoo-ha?"

And I did. She visited us when I was six or seven, wheeled up in the rain to our front door (by whom? my father?) and carried up the front steps (again, by my father? Impossible to picture). Later, with the door of the powder room ajar, I spied my teenage sister Joyce lifting our emaciated grandmother from the toilet. The old woman was naked from waist to shins. This may be my earliest memory of a vulva.

Perhaps it was this same afternoon that we played Go Fish with Grandma O'Brien on our couch, or rather played at her feet while she smiled distractedly, broadly. She had a broad nose too, like Pop Colwell's, and loose gray skin with a faint witch's mustache. She slept on a squeaking metal cot in our dining room and lit her cigarettes off the kitchen stove. We ate lamb for dinner, it was Easter, and the smell of the meat mingling with her cigarette smoke still makes me queasy to remember.

She must have been in her sixties but she seemed already decrepit. Father moved her into a nursing home on Long Island, an hour or so away, where he never visited her (unless he did so in secret). Both his brothers abandoned her there too, as far as I'm aware.

Once in a while Mother would feel guilty and take us—or a couple of us, or one of us—to visit Grandma, and it would be a dispiriting affair, a disquieting hour, surrounded by geriatrics in their antiseptic recreation room. We'd chat about nothing, or not speak at all. Mother might ask a question about Gertrude's family, about our uncle Brian, for example: "Do you know where Brian lives now?" There were rumors that he'd dodged the draft to Canada, or that he was farming marijuana in the wilds of Northern California.

"I don't ask questions," Gertrude replied, if she replied.

She died alone—infections of one form or another, over many years, until one took hold. Nobody came to the funeral except us. My father didn't speak. A rent-a-pastor eulogized with a standard set of platitudes. It was a bright melting muddy Saturday in March.

At the service Mother asked me to recite a poem that Grandma O'Brien had cherished, and I was astounded. She liked poetry? I climbed to the altar and faced the family and read, "And miles to go before I sleep, / And miles to go before I sleep."

We didn't attend a graveside service. Maybe Father had her cremated. What could she have done to deserve this? I used to wonder.

Losing

A THERAPIST, WHO told me he would have rather been a jazz singer, asked me if my father had ever had any dreams. I didn't know: the question had never occurred to me. Father sometimes mentioned a desire to—for some reason—travel east to west across the breadth of Canada by rail; also a notion that, despite a lack of talent for anything remotely approaching hospitality, he had missed his calling as a hotelier, because he said he suspected that in a previous life he'd been a tavern keeper in some remote locale like James Fenimore Cooper's bluest Adirondacks, hanging his lantern out for wayfarers in the night. But these were fantasies and hardly aspirations.

There may still exist somewhere this photo of my father and mother rowing ashore. Already fleshy, his ineradicable stubble smudging his cheeks, Father slouches on the oars. Mother looks grim in the prow, already disappointed. She shields her eyes with her hand like a salute. A picnic basket rolls open and empty between Father's trousered legs; Mother's calves are bare. The sun glints off the bald patch on Harry's crown though he's in his mid-twenties, or younger.

"He was afraid," Mother would say, "that I could never love

a bald man." (I was shocked to learn, then, that my brute of a father could be afraid of anything.) "But what kind of woman would that make me?" she'd ask, rhetorically.

She laughed with us whenever those Hair Club for Men commercials aired; she smiled when we called and requested a free brochure in his name.

When I was young he would comb over what hair he had left, but soon he arrived at his mature look: the lightly freckled bare scalp, sunburned in summer; a chestnut-colored half-tonsure ruffled with just the lightest wave, snowing slowly white from the sideburns. He refused to wear a toupee, he told Mother and she told us, because the humiliation would be too much.

In high school he wore his hair in a ducktail like a greaser. He played football; when I was in high school, his adolescent face stared dully at me from a faded photo of the 1962 varsity team that hung upon the wall of "jock hall," a sunny raucous corridor linking our high school's gyms. But he must have warmed the bench; he was anything but graceful. Once—and only once that I recall—he took me to a field for a toss of the old pigskin, as fathers and sons do. I threw and he ran jerkily to catch, the football bouncing off his thick hands and knocking his fedora sideways. I felt embarrassed for him.

He'd been musical as a teenager, or interested in music anyway. His brother Brian told me that Harry disc-jockeyed at church and school sock hops, and that his favorite song was, by far, "Kookie, Kookie (Lend Me Your Comb)," a snappy pop duet sung by TV stars Edd Byrnes and Connie Stevens.

On long drives in his thirties and forties he might sing along to John Denver, a singer the rest of us loathed, Mother included, for his saccharine, hypocritical (we could tell) faux folk: "Hold me like you'll never let me go," in that reedy voice our father could ape so convincingly. Or he would whistle as he drove, one long piercing tone—mechanical, like an emergency signal—for no reason.

"My father is Buddy Holly," I told friends, and I believed it. He'd looked the part as a teenager. I'd seen pictures.

Of course he couldn't be Buddy Holly, who'd died in a plane crash in a blizzard in 1959 when my father was fourteen; the age I was when I discovered the Beatles, after Joyce, home from college, bought me a *Sgt. Pepper's* cassette on Central Avenue in Yonkers, and I played it on my boom box (what Father referred to as my "ghetto blaster") until the tape snapped.

But he didn't care for those girlie Beatles; Johnny Cash was a "degenerate," and Bob Dylan was for twerps.

In good moods he might listen to his *American Graffiti* soundtrack, especially Del Shannon's tough-guy falsetto on "Runaway," and I'd picture my father at eighteen and nineteen crying in the rain for his runaway—our mother, presumably, who'd run away to college in Michigan.

Through the 1980s he was obsessed with Laura Branigan's "Gloria," rocking in his easy chair by the stereo, staring hungrily at her photo on the album cover: those black leather jeans and red silk blouse, her dark tresses reminiscent of our mother's hair, if only Mother's weren't so coarse and curly. He'd stand to lift the needle, set it down, then sit again and rock.

Crystal Gayle singing "Don't It Make My Brown Eyes Blue," and anything by Linda Ronstadt, and Susan Raye's "L.A. International Airport" (which gave me early on, I swear, a frisson of presentiment as to where I'd one day live); clearly my father had a thing for stormy brunettes. He would be their rock, their protector. He had rescued his runaway, hadn't he? My mother ran back to him, dropping out of college, pregnant with my sister. Their premature marriage was a rescue too in that it removed my mother from the ordeal of her family, promising a new, perfectible family of their own creation.

But the optimism didn't last. Driving along during a summer vacation he inserted a Righteous Brothers cassette and played "You've Lost That Loving Feeling," rewound it, played it again. And again. This was comical, and cruel; this was for her. Our mother turned away from him, from us, stared out the window at the glaring bright dunes rising around us, the seagulls above reeling and crying.

She had had to twist his arm to get him to take some time off. Otherwise he'd have worked himself into an early grave, he claimed. On our way to a rented house in Vermont, bugs spattering the windshield, he'd pull off I-95 in Mystic for a McDonald's milkshake—for himself; his special treat. Or halfway home from the Hedges, a Victorian lodge in the Adirondacks, he'd park our Caprice Classic on the side of the road—a quiet country carriageway—and leave us behind, Mother up front and the whole litter of us sweating in back and the nauseous wayback, as he strolled away along an over-grown path into the shade of a drowsy sun-dappled woods. When he returned, he would have filled his stainless-steel can-teen with water from a spring. He must have remembered this place from his childhood, when he'd visit his uncle near these parts and go hiking and fishing. (My father wasn't an outdoorsy type, but there was an afterglow of such manly—or boyish—pursuits about him.) He sat at the wheel in our parked car again, sipping his spring water. It was so pure, and colder than cold, I remember, so he must have allowed us to taste it, though that seems out of character. This is why the memory has remained vivid for me—that confusion.

———

I have almost no pictures from my childhood. Those I happened to possess when my parents disowned me are loose
and creased in boxes and desk drawers. Like this one of my
father with his sons on the Outer Cape, oceanside, judging
by the height and pitch of the dunes: we're digging together,
a hole like we often dug in the yard in search of ruptured
pipes. There's no anguish apparent in this out-of-focus shot.
Paul squats with his shoulders strong and tan, dredging damp
sand with cupped hands. Chubby Steven sports a baseball cap
and a three-quarters-sleeve jersey. I'm leaping beside them in
a whirl of pallor, all rib cage and femur and crow-black hair,
as if boastful—of my youth, of my athleticism, of being my
mother's favorite?

My father confronts the camera in his prescription sunglasses
and bucket hat (crucial for shielding his baldness from burns),
arms held out from his sides like a plumber at work, or a surgeon after hand-washing for surgery or—better still—after the
surgery, dripping blood. Perhaps playing with his children was
like manual labor to him, and like surgery. (I'll admit I often
find myself holding my arms similarly, unthinkingly, as if I
might contaminate my body with the germs and bacteria of
whatever I've been touching.) My mother must have taken the
photo. They'd been shouting the night before—about money
for the rental house?—while we listened, wide-awake and silent
in our strange beds.

Those summers on the Cape we would laugh with Mother
behind Father's back, while he built his Hoover Dams of sand.
Why this same structure, over and over? Aside from the obvi-
ous: the Lake Mead of his repressed emotions (and libido?),
the strangled Colorado of his career.

I would compete with him, subtly, staking out my plot and with my plastic pail and dinky plastic shovel producing high mounds of sand from which I would carve a megalopolis like Machu Picchu, a hodgepodge of pyramids and ziggurats and terraces for Lilliputian cliff dwellers, all riddled with compulsively coiling staircases. Bathers passing by would pause to admire my city planning, while nearby Father was sculpting his pile into a nearly vertical slab like concrete, smoothing down dam walls with the sole of a flip-flop, patting and sweeping the surrounding beach like a mason or tiler, crawling on his knees backward toward the incoming tide. Nobody dared step close.

After lunch he'd unfurl his nylon box kite and launch it alone, unwinding the twine as he drifted along a dune, the kite's orange panels flapping high above our heads. If he placed the wooden paddle in my hands, I would feel the wax line pulled taut like a wire, as if held at the other end by our Father in heaven.

Most trips to the Cape took place after Paul's suicide attempt had effectively exempted him from all familial obligations. Soon Joyce was pursuing a graduate degree in teaching at Harvard (where she learned that she did not, in fact, want to be a teacher), and Steven had by then escaped to the University of Virginia, followed quickly by a computing job and marriage. I found myself in my teen years the eldest of three—their "second family," as Mother would say with no small amount of self-pity, as if her first three children had failed her, or she'd failed them.

Rainy days we drove to Wellfleet, where women with buzz cuts held each other's hands while browsing the antique shops, or licking their ice cream cones wading into the lazy bayside waves together as the clouds dispersed and burned away. We detested these interminable afternoons. The way Father walked:

Mother would lag behind to make us laugh, mimicking his lordly, ambling stride. We'd jingle the bell on an art gallery's door as if we were genuine collectors, then just stand there appraising sculptures and paintings for what felt like hours. Out of these silences Father might ask me what I thought of *Salt Marsh at Sunset* or *Dolphin Breaching the Bay*. Was he testing me? "I like it," I'd say, "I guess," while Mother, like mothers everywhere, would opine about the more abstract work: "My children can paint better than this." A few times I thought Father was about to buy something; but inevitably he'd just lead us back out the door, with a nod for the attendant, as if we were discerning and not pretending.

He dragged our Christmas tree through the snow in the backyard, hoping to rinse it of urine. Nobody else smelled it. We'd been hoodwinked, he was convinced, but it was too late now for returns. The snow-rinse didn't work. Nothing to do but hacksaw a sapling in the side yard, prop it in the corner of our living room and burden its twigs with a smattering of decorations.

Mother would warn us: "This Christmas will be different." We'd be disappointed, she knew, because other families, our friends' families, had money. We held a lottery, wrote our names on scraps of paper, folded and swished inside Father's fedora, and agreed to adhere to a strict price limit. As for Santa, we were welcome to submit requests, "But I can't make any promises," she'd say, wisely.

The day before Christmas our father would accuse our mother of stinginess—in private, but she'd tell us what he'd said. She moped around the house, smiling wanly, chuckling hollowly, while Father put on a show of holiday merriment—"Jingle, jingle!"—until out the door he'd go shopping (something he never did on any other day); then home again bearing bright crinkling bags from Lord & Taylor, loaded with gifts bought quickly and without consideration: turtlenecks, sweaters, socks. Electric razors for the teenage boys. A Velcro wallet. Nothing fancy but enough to bolster the appearance of a Christmas bounty. Knowing what I know now of his financial limitations, he must have dug himself yearly a deep hole of debt.

Why did he act like this? Was it guilt? Most likely he was thinking of himself. He must have felt deprived on Christmas mornings in his childhood, his brothers plied with treasures; or nobody received many gifts, and he was irked by the working-class meanness of his origins. Who knows the reason, but each Christmas it was evident to us that he was trying to refute something, some unforgivable and irreparable injury.

He was wholly without friends, and as I grow older I have begun to sympathize: the necessary solitude of writing aside, I have always been comfortable letting friends go. Men have trouble with friendship—that's my excuse. Especially if, like me, you don't happen to like men much.

In the summer we might make a day trip to see Amsy and Lee, my father's cousin and his wife in Pearl River. They had an aboveground pool. Father tossed bocce balls and horseshoes in the grass with Amsy and other anonymous kin. Not far from there, as teenagers, he and Amsy used to go night-fishing for eels. Amsy was bald now like my father, with thick glasses too, but mustached. I can't recall them ever throwing their arms around each other, or swapping dirty jokes.

Nobody was worthy of my father's friendship, it seemed. He'd criticize our neighbors and the parents of our friends; he'd inveigh against the Jews and the rich, and the rich Jews in particular. WASPs were only marginally more acceptable because they were so reserved. Everybody was patronizing him, he was sure of it, for his passel of kids, for being Irish Catholic, though he'd only been raised that way, and he never seemed to care about his heritage.

At a dinner party Mr. Bryant spiked somebody's coffee with an olive pit. "Idiot," Father grumbled on his way through our front door; "Never again will I attend a dinner party!" or words to that effect. I wouldn't be surprised to learn that it was my father's slurping lips and tongue that had teased out the unpardonable insolence of that olive pit.

I would have liked to have other fathers. Like tall, handsome, loose-limbed Mr. Davis from the Bronx, with his tales of the bullying Zerega Avenue Oval Boys, now a Manhattan banker married to Susan, an ophthalmologist. Or that trickster Mr. Bryant, who one Labor Day taught me to swim in the "intermediate pool" (his son Tim already knew how): "Kick your legs like a frog," he said; the simile unlocked things for me, and I squirted forward in an epiphany of flotation.

My father had no patience for a phone or a doorbell ringing during dinner. He never let us invite friends over; he needed quiet for working, reading, napping. We had to leave the house for fun.

He hardly ever left the house, though. His leafy-green Raleigh bike rusted in the rear of the garage. He went out walking alone in the evenings after dinner when the weather was good, with his shoulder-high walking stick like a suburban Merlin, donning his fedora or, when the mood struck, a Tyrolean hat with a red Alpine feather in the band. Or Mother accompanied him, and they discussed arcane matters like which children currently required his intercessional castigation. Randomly he might invite one of us along, something we dreaded, the walk but also the invitation: How could we refuse him without revealing again how we feared and disliked him?

The silence while we walked was torturous. So I asked him questions about science to fill the vacuum. He pointed to a house where one of his classmates had grown up, informing me casually that the boy had been killed in Vietnam and his mother had lost her mind. In another house, he said, a Yale student had bludgeoned a sleeping girlfriend to death with a hammer. On these walks my neighborhood, which had been his neighborhood too growing up, was revealed to me as haunted—or haunting, anyway.

He never spoke to the Horniks, the neighbors on our left at the bottom of our dead-end street, beside the brook that fed the swamp. Because he didn't talk to them, we didn't either. Before I was born, or before memory, there had been a falling out—words said or unsaid, behavior that offended my father. The vinyl shade on his side of the bed remained drawn day and night; otherwise he would have had to look out on the Horniks' driveway and, within spitting distance, the window of the garage apartment where the eldest Hornik boy lived. Douglas Jr. or Dougie was "an idiot" (of course) who threw house parties when his parents were out of town. Dougie used drugs, and my father supposed he was a drug dealer too. He tinkered with his IROC-Z in the driveway, his radio polluting our weekend afternoons with Lynyrd Skynyrd, Led Zeppelin, Def Leppard . . .

My father despised them all: Mrs. Hornik with her "hatchet face," and her equally unlovely daughter Nancy (that she shared our mother's name was something we children found bizarre, and humorous); Nicholas the acid freak, in his tie-dyes and Birkenstocks; and lastly sweet-tempered Samuel who was assuredly, in Father's estimation, "a pansy." Mr. Hornik, president of the bank downtown (had he denied my father a loan? was that why?) and a rumored Vietnam vet, was rarely heard but often seen grilling steaks and burgers, shirtless with a can of beer in his hand, his cigar ashing into the gray carpeting of his chest and beer belly. It wasn't long before he died of a heart condition in his early fifties.

We ignored them and they ignored us, side by side in our backyards with only our unpainted, rotting picket fence between. If a ball bounced onto their grass, one of us would have to retrieve it, hopping over and back again as quick as could be. If the Horniks were home then we'd leave it where it lay, sometimes for weeks, watching as the days and the weather leached our ball of color and air. If the Horniks were outside—which was seldom, as both our families seemed preternaturally skilled at evading each other—they might toss our ball back without a word.

And in our front yard too, we'd weed and rake and scoop up clippings beside Father while the Horniks in their yard did the same. If one of them parked a car in front of our house—perturbing Father to no end—and stepped into the street just beyond our hedge, we'd set our faces like stone and look right through them.

If the Horniks were damnable, then the neighbors on our other side were saintly. The Sawyers' house was plain, but Father said they were rich, and their lack of ostentation only impressed him further. Ned Sawyer was Bishop of the local Church of Jesus Christ of Latter-Day Saints; he worked as a life insurance executive in Newark. While the Horniks went unacknowledged, we'd call time-outs from our games to wave and cry "Hello, Mr. Sawyer!" as he returned from work in his chauffeur-driven town car.

The Sawyers had five grown children, dispersed far and wide. Ned's wife Holly presented herself as a model of western femininity (the Sawyers hailed from Wyoming); in her pastel velour tracksuits she was mild, pleasant, plump. She drove a powder-blue Buick Regal with a box of tissues on the dash, and she didn't refrigerate her butter. She took care of us the afternoon of Mother's miscarriage, sending us home with hamburger soup in her thermos.

Father went halfsies with Mr. Sawyer on new gravel for our driveways. They conferred across the Sawyers' low thorn hedge about the latest scourge of Japanese beetles, how to kill garden slugs with saucers of beer, which chemicals Ned sprayed on his Bunyanesque beefsteak tomatoes and lush green lawn. When I fell out of a dogwood tree across the street, Mr. Sawyer ran to me with a fatherly sympathy I'd never seen before.

Ned Sawyer inspired our father to be a better man, and we welcomed two blond missionaries in their white shirts, black ties, and baggy black suits into our home to discuss the Book of Mormon around the dining room table. At their urging our father filled our basement with provisions of rice, honey, wheat, yeast, and powdered milk in Tupperware buckets, retrofitting the room where he kept his model train set into a makeshift bomb shelter—for emergencies, Father said, like hurricanes and nuclear winter.

We started attending the Sawyers' church, praying with them in their curiously narcoleptic manner, heads bowed and arms folded. I introduced myself to the Sunday-school class as Steve Austin, Six-Million-Dollar Man, and demonstrated my bionic powers by running in slow motion around the common table. They seemed to accept me.

But Father reconsidered. He was a contrarian, he said—a free thinker, in his way; and Mother didn't care for the church's sexism, as she saw it, how a man's wife or, worse still, wives would die and find themselves sentenced to that moon or planet or wherever their husbands had been sent for all eternity. This was the only time I remember Mother siding with "the women's-libbers," a deplorable group in her opinion who were, by and large, judging her harshly as a worthless housewife.

The truth is that my parents, and my father in particular, got cold feet. A congregation—any community of any kind—was beyond him.

He had trouble finishing things. The cabinet meant to conceal our TV and stereo in the living room remained topless and unstained. His "marble monster," an in-process octopus of wooden rollways, collected dust and spiders beneath our basement stairs. The shower in the bathroom was permanently broken; we'd squat at the spout to wet our hair with our hands, splash our pits, bickering before and after about who'd left the latest gray ring of scum.

He couldn't devise a workable system or contraption for securing our garbage cans from the hordes of racoons who came rampaging nightly through out backyard. With a high-powered slingshot and shiny ball bearings he brained some raccoons one evening; but these were recalcitrant critters. Another evening he beckoned us to the window to watch as he lit a firecracker and dropped it in the mouth of a can he'd left open; the flash then pop, and a fat raccoon came scrabbling out, shaking the din from its ears, staggering in circles in the grass before, undeterred, it clambered back inside. He sent us all to bed.

Past midnight he perched like Lee Harvey Oswald in the kitchen window with his .22 rifle, and he shot the raccoons. Or shot at them: a shape shrieked like a cat. He came to bed and told Mother that he would have to apologize to the Fitzgeralds first thing in the morning for accidentally assassinating their tabby. It was the honorable thing to do.

At dawn he saw he'd been wrong: it was a raccoon, after all. Two, in fact, an adult and a juvenile, both still breathing but immobile in the cinders beside our charcoal grill. He woke Paul and told him to collect the Louisville Slugger from the garage. When Paul came around to the backyard, Father commanded him to bludgeon the raccoons. But he wouldn't do it, or he couldn't, Paul told me years later, so our father was forced to finish the job.

In my pajamas I watched from the window above: Father's baldness bent low, the baseball bat cocked. I don't remember the blows, the sound or sight of the skulls crushed.

Steven and I helped them dig the holes beside the wood-pile on the side of the house. Then we covered the raccoons with the dirt. A fine new grass grew on their graves, but no matter how much time passed the earth underfoot felt soft and sinking.

When friends and friends' parents asked what our father was, we'd say: "Computers." His business cards and stationery indicated an office that didn't exist in White Plains. Our kitchen telephone had two lines, and if he was downstairs when his line rang (an infrequent event) he would answer professionally, with that gentle, colorless tone he could acquire, a performance that never failed to impress me. We'd have to keep quiet while he talked, pretending we weren't where he was.

One time I noticed him through the glass of the door to his attic office and he was just sitting there, motionless, staring at the empty desk before him, hands in his lap, beneath his two skylights in what was now the coolest room in the house, thanks to a new AC unit. (While Joyce slept across the hallway in her garret like Cinderella, waking up summer mornings in a brain-poached stupor.)

Mother explained he was meditating—"for the stress," she said. This was uncharacteristically Eastern of him, hippieish, like something he'd read about in one of his Joseph Campbell books.

Paul told me that our father would play solitaire on his computer all day long. Paul knew this because he worked for him for a while, after flunking out of college, two years after jumping from the window in the very room where now he played solitaire too, a few feet away across the beige commercial carpeting from Father. Together they were supposed to be developing a new billing software for beverage distributors. Paul told me that nobody bought it.

And yet the myth of our father's formidable intellect endured. His prodigious math-and-science mind. He could have been a computer engineer, Mother often said, "the next Bill Gates," if only things had broken his way. And I suppose he did have a certain technical acumen. He foretold (it haunts me still) that by "the year 2000" everybody would read letters, newspapers—even literature—on their computer screens. The whole family rebelled against this prediction one night over dinner. I was straining to suppress tears.

He liked movies, so long as he didn't have to leave the house. When VCRs were new he bought us one, and we'd rent movies downtown by the train station, in a shop with a walk-in closet where they kept the pornographic films. (My father claimed he saw Mr. Connolly from up the street ducking behind the beaded curtain once.) He liked action: *Death Wish*, the *Rambo* trilogy, *Patton*, *Dirty Harry*, *Escape from Alcatraz* (anything with Clint Eastwood, really). We enjoyed these entertainments as a family, or the boys did; he wouldn't stay for the end. For some reason—boredom or excitement, I could never tell which—with act three hurtling into view, our father would stand, unzip, pull his pants down to mid-thigh, smooth his shirttails over his briefs, pull his pants back up to mid-belly, and zip, button, belt. Then off to bed he'd go.

Like Mother he liked books, but his were Del Rey paper-backs, sci-fi and fantasy, or westerns by Louis L'Amour. He collected them in the particleboard bookcase outside his attic office door, along with his VHS tapes of the Battle of Britain and Gulf War highlights. He never borrowed books because he considered libraries to be unhygienic.

Several Saturday evenings in a row he came home with pizza and Pepsi for the boys. We liked computer games so he said, "Let's design our own." Something to do with dragons and elves. We brainstormed around the dining room table far into the night, while he scribbled notes in his yellow legal pad. But nothing came of these sessions. The pads piled up inside his night table, beneath his Trojan condoms and his *Brief History of Time*.

"Your father's a loser," my mother's stepmother Regina told me. "Remember how he'd dress up in a suit and tie and not *go* anywhere?"

We were talking on the phone. I hadn't heard her voice in fifteen years, since my parents had sued her and my mother's siblings regarding my grandfather's will. I'd caught her at her condo at the Westchester Country Club, a nineteenth-century Italianate villa with a polo field, two golf courses, tennis, squash, a beach club on Long Island Sound. Where one evening we children dressed in blazers and ties and picked at our fish in the Biltmore Room. Crystal chandeliers, silver candelabras, ivory tablecloths . . . My hands were shaking as I dialed her number.

"It was just this very 1950s situation. Your mother wanted

to stay home, and your father was going to be the breadwinner," Regina said. "Only problem was: he wasn't winning any
bread!" We both laughed. She told me she was leaving for
Florida in the morning so we'd have to make this quick.

"Everything bad that has happened to your family, Danny,"
she leveled with me, "has had to do with the problem of who
your father truly is."

I was startled. Did she mean what I hoped she meant? I
shared with her my hypothesis, my fantasy probably, only
recently forming, that my father wasn't in fact my father. My
father's younger brother Brian, whom I looked like, whom I
took after temperamentally, who'd disappeared not long after
I was born—was it possible that he was my true father?

She didn't think so. "I think it's too late to change who your
father is," Regina said. "But what do I know? Why don't you
go ask Brian?"

King Brian

I CAN'T PINPOINT the change; after the disowning, before the cancers. I was washing dishes, or walking the dog. I feared I was losing my grip on reality, paranoid like my parents. But it would make so much sense!—and a good story too; it might even make a memoir.

The last day I saw my father he cornered my wife-to-be: "Aren't you embarrassed of him?" he said, meaning me. "He looks like Allen Ginsberg!" Then less anti-Semitically (and homophobically) he uttered quietly: "He looks just like my brother Brian . . ." He meant my full beard and curly hair; but maybe something else. Something repressed was returning to my father, returning for him.

Grandma O'Brien believed, and liked to tell her children and grandchildren, that we were the direct descendants of Brian Boru, eleventh-century high king of Ireland and "Imperator Scottorum," emperor of the Gaels (a popular notion among O'Briens the world over, our mother would remind us). Grandma was the only member of our family who was interested in her roots. But at a young age I discovered that, like her, I felt my Irishness keenly. Their music stirred me. The coils in

Celtic artwork reminded me of the obsessive pattern-seeking of my anxiety, and of my creativity. The Irish propensity for tragedy, often masquerading as comedy, struck me as irrepressible and unbearably poignant.

One Christmas Grandma O'Brien sent me a coffee-table tome about Ireland: vibrant color photographs of pints of peaty stout resting on froths of Kenmare lace, bony pilgrims crawling along stony paths toward shrines or grottoes in places with names like Ballinspittle and Mount Melleray, where schoolgirls had seen a full-bodied Marian apparition, or a statue of the Virgin weeping oil or blood as she inclined her head and rocked the infant savior in her arms.

A single page of this book instilled in my psyche the myth of King Brian. Ascending from southern obscurity, Brian united the fractious chieftains of his generation. On Good Friday of 1014 his warriors drove the invading Danes back into the rising tide of Clontarf Bay outside Dublin, in a storm that intermingled rain with blood and blood with waves. The Viking leader Brodir, reputedly a devotee of the dark arts, transmogrified himself into a crow and flew behind enemy lines where he spied the septuagenarian Brian alone in his camp, down on his knees in prayer. Brodir became a man again, and with his axe swiftly decapitated the emperor of the Gaels. In the morning Brian's son captured Brodir, slit him from navel to neck, and marched him around the trunk of a great ash tree like Yggdrasil, the Dane disemboweling himself with every step until he collapsed on the gory moss, a steaming shell of a man.

As a boy I would imagine—no, I would *see* King Brian in his prime, fiery hair and beard, loping through the swamp across from our house, or galloping on his white steed through scraggly woods alongside the New York State Thruway as we drove. Cracking sticks off trees and sharpening their tips on curbstones, a crude substitute for Brian's steel, I pretended I was him in my games, and if not him then his avenging son.

I was frightened of my fascination; King Brian reminded me of the fantasy novels that my father and brother Paul loved. Their allegiance to the genre struck me as childish, stunted. And then there was the worrisome whiff of the occult about such tales, with their demonic imagery (and energy?), though what was actually scaring me was the occult emotion of despair that my father and brother seemed to embody and repress.

Nevertheless after college I would spend a year backpacking around Ireland because of King Brian, or rather because of an unconscious longing for a feasible father. "Why do you want to go *there*?" my father asked, days before I was to depart. "It's wet. They're poor. We came to this country for a reason." (For him as for multitudes of the diaspora, Ireland remains, as James Joyce memorably phrased it, "the old sow that eats her own farrow"; but Harry wouldn't have known James Joyce from Éamon de Valera.) I couldn't tell anybody why I was going because I didn't fully know myself. My proposal for the fellowship that would send me in search of my fatherland was entitled "Looking for Brian."

Brian O'Brien was wild, a bit screwy. His redundant name had made him that way, my father explained; his left-handedness too: the nuns at Immaculate Heart of Mary would tie his sinister hand behind his back and make him write with his right. "Write with your right!" they would shout, and when they caught him using his left hand they rapped those knuckles raw.

Brian's arrival in the world surprised his parents in their middle age, and they're said to have spoiled him. His mother gave him her maiden name for his middle name. His father took him to Knicks games. Scarsdale High School in the late 1960s was shuddering in the grips of the suburban counterculture, and the teenage Brian shucked his shoes and grew a pony-tail and an *Easy Rider* mustache. He's smiling in his yearbook photo—class of '70, with a gap in his front teeth just like my father; Harry's baby fat too—above a quotation from the Swiss philosopher-aphorist Henri Amiel: "Moral indifference is the malady of the cultivated class." This was how Brian felt about Scarsdale, and how I felt growing up there too.

After his father died Brian moved to Miami with his mother. He burned his draft card, stole his mother's rare coin collection and her car, and drove off the map. Nobody could ever track him down. These scant facts were the seeds of the family myth about him.

My first two memories are of Brian. I'm strapped in a stroller in a living room in the afternoon, looking up a staircase that turns on a landing. Sunlight suffusing gauzy curtains . . . My grandmother sold my father's childhood home on Madison Road not long after I was born; this is that house, I am sure. I'm alone, but somebody is up there above me, above my head, just up the darkening stairs—two voices now. Mother and the other. Speaking, arguing, conspiring like lovers.

In the second memory Brian is smiling down on me. We're in my bedroom. His beard is bushy, his already thinning hair fans along his broad shoulders; he's shambolic, shamanic, like Allen Ginsberg or Jesus. He hands me a children's Bible, then walks downstairs and out the door, never to be seen again.

There had to be a reason. But there wasn't, my mother insisted the few times I found an opportunity to ask. She was baffled. She didn't seem to miss him.

But a reason could answer so much! Why, for example, of all my siblings, I looked the least like my father. Why I was taller, my shoulders broader, my voice deeper. Why I liked people, and hated conformity and dogma. Why I hated Harry and he hated me more.

All it takes is an afternoon, or less. Up the stairs in their mother's house on Madison Road, or in his brother Harry's house, in his brother's marriage bed while Harry was at work (in the days when he still went out to work).

Mother would be twenty-seven, Brian in college. He read books, debated politics. He was sensitive, a natural-born listener, precociously wise and besotted with empathy for this tortured, frustrated, brilliant young woman, my mother. He was so many things Harry could never be.

If only I could find Brian, I thought, I might finally understand why Harry would stare across the dining room table at me as if he didn't know who I was. Or as if he did know.

A private eye in downtown Los Angeles dug up an address for "Brian Colwell O'Brien" after about twenty minutes of Internet sleuthing: my uncle (my father?) was living in Lake Worth in Palm Beach County, Florida. All those years my parents said that he was lost, that he'd left no trace behind—had they even tried? Or they wanted me to believe he was unfindable, so I wouldn't go looking for myself.

My first letter was professional. I sought to impress him with my credentials. I was engaged in the research phase of a book that would concern itself with the history of "the O'Briens of Scarsdale," and would he care to contribute? I included my phone number, along with my street and email and website address.

He didn't call. Or write, or email. But for weeks—then months—somebody in Lake Worth was visiting my website every night. Like most writers I know, I monitor my site's traffic, its dribs and drabs of statistical validation, and every night

"Lake Worth" landed on my "News" page—readings, maybe a play production or a publication in a literary magazine; then Lake Worth might visit the "Contact" page, which provided only a link to my agent in New York. But he would always click on "Biography," the page with my author's photo. Some nights he viewed only that page, as if he'd bookmarked it.

Then, just like that, Lake Worth stopped visiting. Months passed. I tried again and this time I was honest, appealing to his vanity too:

Dear Brian:

I'm writing you another letter because I wasn't entirely truthful with you before. One of my earliest memories is of you looking down on me, giving me a children's Bible the morning you left our house in Scarsdale. But maybe I imagined this? Maybe I imagined you, because the family myth of you, somebody rebellious, politically and artistically inclined, leaving his family behind—all this was something I could identify with, if not aspire to . . .

Three days later he emailed, in ALL CAPS, as if hollering across the chasm of three decades. It read to me, thrillingly, like a telegram from a lunatic asylum:

THANKS FOR THE INVITE TO THE DANCE DANNO. IM HAPPY TO SEE YOU MADE IT PAST THE AGE OF THREE AND DONE SO SPLENDIDLY. I ALWAYS BELIEVED YOUR TALENT FOR COMIC SELF DESTRUCTION HAD SOMETHING TO DO WITH SOME BOISTOROUS JOY AND FEARLESSNESS THAT

HAD YOU GOING DOWN THE WRONG WAY
ON THE STAIRS. HA HA HA. BUMMED TO HEAR
ALL THIS STURM UND DRANG AND BULLSHIT
WITH YOUR FOLKS BUT ITS A RECURRING
THEME IN THIS FAMILY. ENOUGH SAID.
CHUG-N-GO MY AWFULLY WEDDED WIFE
HA HA HA KNEW WHO YOU WERE FROM
THAT PICTURE ON YOUR WEBSITE YOUR
HANDS ARE DEFINITELY OBRIEN HANDS
THESE HANDS UNCLOG DRAINS HAMMER
NAILS GUT FISH THANK GOD YOUR MOMMA
DIDNT HAVE THAT BALDNESS GENE CAUSE IT
WOULDNT FIT A HAUNTED FUCKING IRISH
WRITER! HA HA HA! I HAD A HANDLE ON THE
OBRIEN CLAN LONG TIME PASSING BLUNTLY
SPEAKING MY BIG BROTHER HAROLD IS A
SHIT HEAD FOR LETTING THIS HAPPEN TO
YOU AND YOUR FAMILY WITH CERTAINTY
HE LET THIS HAPPEN!! NO MYTH I AM WHO
YOU HAVE ALWAYS PERCEIVED ME TO BE!!!!!!! I
MARCH TO THE BEAT OF MY OWN DRUM HA
HA HA TIME IS ON MY SIDE IVE GOT SCADS
OF IT TOO SO WHY DONT WE RATTLE THE
BONES WHEN YOU CALL? WITH THE IRISH ITS
A GOOD IDEA TO START WITH ENVY.

The phone call was exhausting. He did most of the talking,
pathologically so, on his cell phone in his pickup driving with
motorcycles buzzing and horns honking somewhere in Florida,
I presume. (He worked freelance all over the country, he said,
in his semiretirement restoring historical homes after a long
career in commercial construction.) He was a cacophonic
laugher, a recovering alcoholic (he just up and quit one day

"with no help from nobody," like his mother did, he said—like I would quit too, a few years after this conversation, though in my case I would need the catalyst of cancer). Still, he smoked; he coughed hard on the line. Also arthritis, and a cataract in need of surgery that accounted for the ALL CAPS (though, energetically speaking, he spoke in ALL CAPS too). His brand of paranoia, his cocky go-it-aloneness—everything felt familiar.

Intriguingly, Brian's wife was, like my mother, also a Nancy, but he called her "Chug-and-Go" without elaboration. Unprompted he offered the observation that my website photo resembled a "more studious version" of himself, and he hooted when I told him that my wife and I jokingly referred to him as "Papa Brian." When asked if he'd ever had children, he said "no, not really . . . but I got about a hundred of them spread out all over the country! *That's* the way to do it, man!" He laughed himself into another coughing fit. Then he fell somber; I heard sirens wailing in the background: "But me and Chug-and-Go like to, you know, adopt kids from time to time, informally, like lost boys and girls—like you, Danny!" And he laughed himself into another paroxysm of hacking and phlegm.

"You've got to understand, Danny, something about your family," he said. "Everything goes back to my childhood."

"*Your* childhood?"

"Because essentially I should've never been born. As this late-in-life baby, aka the Mistake, aka the Gift from God, nobody was going to pay an ounce of attention to the Little Turd. But I was sure as shit going to pay attention to *them*. You follow me?"

"So what you're saying—"

"The greatest gift my family ever gave me was the gift of listening. I thank them every day."

"But—"

"They taught me how to *listen* . . . to see what's *really* going on . . . all around me. And for me, the answer to your question—'What happened to my family?'—is simple: it's your father, Danny. It's your father."

That's when he called Harry a psychopath, as I'd long described him to friends, with some embarrassment because he wasn't physically violent; but those dead eyes, empty of all empathy . . . "Both of your parents, come to think of it, are psychopaths. And you must never forget what psychopaths do: they don't always kill with bullets. They don't always slit your throat. They deprive. They shame. They tear your heart out of your chest, look at it, and stick it back in the wrong way. They do everything but pull the trigger. And you know why? Because they're scared they're going to lose you."

"Well they've lost me now," I said.

"Have they?"

He felt sorry for Harry: "The reason your father wound up an angry peckerhead has everything to do with a rocky transition at age fourteen from the working-class Irish and Italians of Immaculate Heart of Mary to Scarsdale High School's maelstrom of affluence and achievement." Also big brother Johnny's popularity—Harry just couldn't compete. But Brian had another insight to share, something he knew I'd find shocking.

"Harry wanted to be a writer. Oh yeah! *Oh* yeah! He loved *Beowulf*, and he could be very sensitive, you had to be very careful around Harry because his perceptual screens were all fucked up. *All* fucked up . . ." As for himself, Brian had aspired to become a "head shrink" one day, he told me, but early on he discovered with disappointment that he was too sensitive, and "empathy's a real liability in the mental health field." Like his brother he'd also considered becoming a writer but "I wouldn't have been able to stomach all that backslapping and backstabbing—the politics, man!" Harry had hoped to write fantasy and science-fiction novels specifically; the postapoc-alyptic *A Canticle for Leibowitz* had been his Bible as a teen. (Brian couldn't believe I'd never heard of this book before— "It's a God damned classic!") He said: "He's jealous of you, Danny. You're a writer with a website and everything." But his brother should have remained who he was, a man born to work with his hands, a plumber or a builder like Brian and the countless generations of useful O'Briens before them.

I was surprised to hear him speak tenderly of camping with my father at Uncle Marv's lake upstate: "Harry loved that lake more than anybody." And in that moment I recalled a photo of these brothers side by side, brandishing a brace of fish for the camera. Harry was kind to Brian there, hunting and fishing, before Uncle Marv had to sell the land. Their father couldn't afford to buy it, Brian said, and Harry resented once again their old man's shortcomings. Harry lost his lake around the time he met my mother.

And Brian didn't hold back about her either: Nancy was "the type of person you'd back away from if she had a knife in her hand," as well as a "hot sweaty mess, producing children en masse—not part of my territorial imperative, if you know what I mean."

"Why did you just disappear?" I asked. We'd been on the phone for hours; I didn't know if I'd ever have this chance again.

"I didn't disappear. I disappeared from your family—there's a difference."

"Okay. But why?"

"I'll tell you when it happened. It was after your father went into business for himself. After they rented him an office in that fancy-ass building downtown in Scarsdale, where Harry was supposed to be a corporate captain-of-industry type now. Like Nancy's dad. And with Nancy's father's money too, by the way—that's how they were paying the rent. Well . . . I just knew all that bullshit was going to hit the fan one day. It's like my second mother, Esther Weiss, used to say: 'Keep your tsuris out of someone else's backyard.' You follow me? Because it was clear your parents had enough tsuris of their own."

"Was my mother's father paying for everything? Was that the problem in my family?"

"No! You think? You genius!"

"Right . . ."

"I'm just being flippant with you here, Danny . . . I know. I know . . . Sometimes the hardest thing to figure out is what's staring you right in the face. Things having to do with your family."

"Right."

"You wrote that you had a question for me? Something more important than the other questions? About me?"

"Right."

"So hit me."

"I think you answered everything."

"Did I?"

"Yeah, no—everything makes sense now."

"You sure?"

I don't know why I didn't ask him. He hung up. I didn't want to scare him away; I didn't want to give up—I still don't want to give up—the dream. I like to think that one day, however unlikely, Brian will write or call to confess that yes, I am right, I was always right, I have always known who my true father is.

Some months after he sent me that photo album of my grandmother's adolescence, I emailed and asked him for a photo of himself, and he didn't respond. He hasn't responded since, not even after I let him know about my cancer. According to the internet his house has been sold. He may be dead.

That day on the phone he had some parting words for me that feel like wisdom as the years pass: "Look, you've had some rough shakes in life. Nobody's going to deny that. But the way I see it, you can see life as like a sorrowful negative, like Oh poor me! and Why did my parents do this to me? Or you go: You know what? That wasn't easy, but I got something out of it. I got to grow up in Scarsdale. I got to go to college. I'm alive. I get to get up every day and write poems and plays and bullshit . . .

"When I think about the good and the bad I've had in *my* life . . . ? It's *mine*, baby! I *own* this pain! Nobody's going to take that away from me . . .

"Because listen: I got lucky. You want the truth, Danny? Of course you do . . . I got lucky the moment I walked out your family's front door. You follow me?"

III. My Escape

Iterations

UNLATCHING THE GATE pinched our fingers. So we'd straddle the black banister in the hallway above, swing our feet to the wood as it curved and sloped away—then dismount into our bounding jailbreaks.

An olive-colored carpet ran down the middle of the stairs, tacked into paint-spotted planks. Watercolor warblers behind glass in wooden frames hung diagonally along the wall, blinding with flashes of sunlight from an open bedroom door above.

We knew who was descending: Mother, hushed and rhythmic in a rush going nowhere, her ankle clicking, arms hugging laundry for the basement, novels and self-help books to be returned to the library. Father lumbering steadily, his knee clicking, shushing the banister beneath his soft sliding paw. Joyce, the nervous eldest, quiet like a phantom parachutist; Paul prancing, almost a gallop; and Steven's sloppy free fall, which Mother liked to tease him for. She would tease us all. The way we came downstairs was too revealing.

I don't remember what I sounded like. I remember trying to sound like nobody.

———

Once upon a time Danny was the youngest of three brothers. The third prince solves the riddle, slays the beast. Shakespeare's third suitor is the one worthy of love, at least romance. The third son in the old world, never to inherit his father's land, nor preordained for the priesthood, left kith and kin to seek his fate across the wine-dark sea.

I liked to walk down our dead-end street imagining I was returning from war, from Europe, from the coast of Bohemia, a sack slung over my world-weary shoulders; through the front door I saw myself bursting, spilling the bounty of my experience at my family's feet, proving to them at long last my value.

During the day when the others were at school, I thrilled to climb the stairs to Joyce's attic room, with its sunflower-yellow walls and a hard-backed poster of a '60s songstress, strumming her guitar in a field of blurry buttercups. I ransacked her dollhouse like a fat-fingered god, upsetting Lilliputian furniture, scattering the minuscule clay steaks and corn cobs and fruit, while playing her records: Glenn Campbell's "Rhinestone Cowboy," Abba's "Voulez-Vous" for the danger of lyrics that seemed to have something to do with sex. I told my mother that "violins sound like love," and she prophesied again, "You will be a poet."

Joyce was seven years older than me, so old that I felt she could have been my mother. She indulged me. When I couldn't sleep, I would beg her to sit on the foot of my bed in her nightgown and wait, and she did. When she felt sad, which was normal enough, she would seat herself at the upright piano in the dining room and plonk away at the *Great Songs of the Sixties: Vol. 1*, at half speed due to her technical limitations, singing

"Bridge over Troubled Water," for instance, in her lamenting (and lamentable) high-church style.

Choosing between two older brothers, Paul was the one I could admire: with his collared shirts buttoned high and his blond hair shimmering in a silken bowl cut, lightly feathered, slightly Californian. He launched his toy rockets on dusty baseball diamonds. He snapped and glued his model airplanes. He understood electronics. He was smart and seemed to tolerate my company.

Steven was his "Irish twin," a year or so younger, dark-haired and oafish, a thick-lipped pouter and scowler, a left-handed moper and stooper in his ubiquitous jeans jacket. A dedicated viewer of Saturday-morning wrestling, and the kung fu flicks that followed. Steven was tough, or wanted to be. One day when I was out sick, a Japanese classmate brought my homework around; Steven arrived at my bedside: "Some chink told me to give this to you," before tearing the mimeographed pages into confetti that he sprinkled in my lap.

He didn't like me because we shared a room. He slept with his pillow at his footboard so he wouldn't have to see me, across the floor in my bed, with my pillow against my headboard so I could see him. I needed to see him coming, because he liked to start his day by twisting my arm, a ritual he only abandoned after I cut my scalp on the windowsill one morning, writhing away from his grasp. Twirling me around in the supermarket's meat aisle, he popped my elbow out of its socket. Another time he launched a bulky metal action figure into the air, and as it fell it sliced my head open, requiring stitches (to this day I retain a faint inch-long scar along my hairline).

He slept with his hands down his pants, as if possessive and protective. When he dressed he pulled his shirt down over his penis and scrotum and, to be fair, I followed suit. We never saw each other naked.

Because I found it humorous, I told everybody that Steven swore himself to sleep, for that's what it sounded like—a grumbling, whispering rendition of Father's spluttering tirades of "shit" and "piss" while snaking drains and dredging gutters. Maybe these weren't actually swear words and Steven was, in some fashion, like me in my bed, praying? Looking back I can see he was an anxious kid: folding his clothes after he'd worn them in neat piles on the floor; nightly arranging his figurines like troops in serried ranks before his bed, facing out in defense—of what? Me? Perhaps he was jealous of me, though I was three and a half years younger. I was passably popular at school, I was athletic, I was Mother's youngest (for the time being). He'd write in a spidery hand on the ceiling above my bed: "Shrimp!" and "Teeny-weeny!" and other belittling taunts. He Scotch-taped his *Sports Illustrated* covers to the walls in his corner—Mike Tyson, Michael Jordan, and two dozen more— and when I was out of the room he would rearrange them, only to deny later what he'd done. I was going crazy, he would say, laughing, and so did everybody in the family laugh about the mind games Steven was playing with me.

Paul fought Steven only once, like a Gilgamesh to Steven's wild man Enkidu, or an abler Abel besting a clumsy Cain, punching and kicking and rolling through the gravel and broken bottle glass of the cul-de-sac we called the turnaround. Then side by side they stood chastised by Mother in the front hallway, bloodied, tears streaking the dirt on their cheeks. Had somebody pulled them apart? We were not a physical family; it was hard to believe something as marvelous as a fistfight could occur.

Steven would have his revenge. One evening he placed a pair of underpants across the burning bulb of Paul's bedside lamp. Soon the briefs caught fire. Mother cried "Out! Out!"

and we raced outside, ducking behind the privet hedge as, from the stoop, storm door crashing wide, she hurled Paul's flaming lamp into the dewy night.

Mother was cruelest to Steven. She twisted around in the driver's seat at the red light one rainy afternoon and slapped his face. Her fingernails drew blood from his cheek.

One morning she followed us to school shouting, determined to work the teeth of a black comb through Steven's unruly russet waves. She yanked and jabbed, eyes rolling, mouth a sneer. She rode his back like a goblin or witch, as he lumbered mulishly onward, onward, his brothers and sisters and schoolmates gawking, spellbound. This was the day he ran away. But the police returned him by dinnertime. He'd been hiding in the rocks at school. I watched from our shared room as an officer opened the back door of the patrol car, and Steven stepped sheepishly out, then Mother sweeping down the stoop to kneel on the slate of the walk and embrace her son with a passion I'd never seen before, and would never see again.

Everybody agreed: I wasn't like them, my siblings. Even less like my father. I was forever being told I was like my mother, and her father especially.

"You're a bullshit artist, like he is," Father informed me. (It was some consolation that he was thinking of me as an artist at all.) But I did not understand why my Welsh-ness offended him. How was I to know how he disliked his father-in-law, how they disliked—even despised—one another? The truth was that my grandfather considered my father to be the lifelong mistake his teenage daughter had made; so in retaliation my father would—at least in private—condemn his father-in-law as a fake, a conniver who thrived because of his presumed immorality.

Grandpa Welsh sewed bricks of cash into a full-length winter coat and flew, sweating, to the Caymans to help out a golfing buddy in a jam, for instance. So he was a bullshit artist, and more than a bit crooked. (But what success isn't?) Whereas Harry, self-described "straight shooter," was forever feeling himself maltreated by dishonest men. And I was complicit in the world's corruption in my father's eyes whenever I seemed to succeed.

"You walk like my father," my mother would say. "The same determined stride. Not everybody likes his stride, you know—your directness and force. You have his hair too. You and I both have his curls. My hair was too curly as a girl, like one of the Three Stooges—not 'Curly' but 'Larry.' The kids called me 'Larry' as a tease. Your grandfather's curls he'd slick back with pomade each morning, and if he didn't then his head would explode in a kinky mess like Dylan Thomas. And my maiden name is 'Welsh,' like Dylan Thomas—get it? We're Welsh, you and I! We have Welsh hair! And your eyes are my father's too, Danny . . . Such dreamy bedroom eyes. You have a way with people. They like you. Like him, you are destined to succeed."

In my heart I felt orphaned like my grandfather had been. An only child too. I didn't know why I felt this way. I had parents, I had siblings. There was no denying them.

Our father said we shouldn't speak like the children we were, these children they kept having like children themselves—he of the perpetual adolescent fury. But Mother couldn't or wouldn't speak otherwise, as if she were still the girl she was when she fell pregnant with Joyce; or younger, the age at which she was most formatively abused.

When she visited her mother-in-law in that nursing home on Long Island, they would chat affectionately like acquaintances; as time went on, then, like amiable strangers, thanks to the senile dementia infantilizing Grandma O'Brien's brain. When something the old woman said made no sense, my mother would reply, "Oh yes, isn't that nice?" Theirs became a childish conversation in the clinical sense.

As soon as she was home from these visits Mother would beg us, her children, "Don't lock me away like that when I'm old. Though I know you will anyway, I know you will forget me . . ." Like a child who knows she will—she must—be punished, she foresaw a future when few would care for her, few if any of her children who grew up speaking childishly, our natural voices strangled in our throats and smothered on our lips. The voices of sad men and madwomen.

Will my daughter wish for siblings—these genetic iterations of herself—to emulate and rival and repudiate? Will she miss her chance to feel embarrassed or miffed when a neighbor or a cousin mistakes her again for her sister or her mother?

I hope she will know that we tried—for her sake, and for our own; because we had wanted to at least make the choice for ourselves.

Her mother was diagnosed at thirty-eight—there was no time to waste. They would harvest her eggs the morning after her double mastectomy and simultaneous breast reconstruction surgery. I drove her at dawn from the hospital in Beverly Hills to the clinic in Redondo Beach and a doctor who appeared on reality TV. My wife was sedated but groaning, cursing at me when I took a sharp turn, or hit a bump or a pothole. An oxygen tank clanked in the back seat (in case she had trouble breathing). My cramping was racking; I was unwittingly closing in on my own diagnosis. An attractive, yawning young nurse ushered me into a brightly lit closet with a wipeable recliner and

a flat-screen TV (cycling through soft-focused photos of foun-
tains and flowers) where she told me to "use the plastic cup."
We would do this again several weeks later, just before she was
to begin chemotherapy treatment (after treatment, drugs meant
to prevent recurrence would induce an early menopause). Both
times only two or three eggs were fertilized, and both times
nothing took. I wasn't disappointed. I had long had a feeling
that our daughter would be our one and only.

The evening after her birth, her mother was asleep when
two grandmotherly nurses instructed me to accompany her,
all ten pounds of her, so that she might smell me and know
that I was near as they rolled her down a corridor into an ICU
of sick and premature newborns—though she wasn't ill, and
the opposite of underweight; they just needed their supplies.
I couldn't understand how they could stick a needle in something so tiny, so finely exquisite. It was "standard procedure,"
they assured me, and my daughter wasn't bothered. She didn't
cry. She knew I was there by her side.

Buried

IN THE OLD nightmares, before I left them or they left me (both are true), I am buried alive. Soil and snakes and roots and worms suffocate me—I wake wrecking the shades, clawing at curtains, hands pressed to the cool of windowpanes.

More recently my mother pursues me, sometimes with Father and my sisters in tow, through a recital hall or a theater after a poetry reading I've given or the performance of a play I've written about them; they're enraged, or mystified and aggrieved, seeking explanation for my cruelty, calling my name through crosscurrents of crowds. I somehow get away.

In my dreams lately I have never left home. I'm as old as I am now; my mother is what she was then and will always be. We are converging. I recall everything that's changed between us, in this dream that is not quite a nightmare, but she's forgotten all, or she never knew. I don't know why I'm there, what spell keeps bringing me home.

Her hold on me has felt, at times, like witchcraft—a curse of some kind, surely. My good luck cannot last. When our daughter was born healthy, my wife healthy too, I felt that we had slipped through my mother's net.

Just after we'd bought our first home in California, my

mother sent me and my wife a condolence card (how did she find our unlisted address? and so quickly?) that depicted a charcoal Rorschach of a dove in flight above a manufactured message that read: "With each memory we meet again with those we love . . . for the heart never forgets." And more preprinted cursive: "With love and prayers and thoughts of you," signed in loopy ballpoint, "Love, Mom and Dad"—her handwriting, not my father's.

Nobody had died. She was, whether she knew it or not, cursing us again. Three years later when the cancers hit, I felt foolish to have believed I could ever be free.

She never wrote or called again. In the hospital for thirteen days, with a tube up my nose and down my throat into my stomach, my stitched-up colon leaking into my abdomen, my bladder spurting through a drainage hole in my side, I worried helplessly that my family might appear at my bed. I needn't have worried. None of them showed up.

I believed I was her favorite because she told me. "Don't tell the others," she would whisper, "or they will be jealous."

A therapist, elderly and wraithlike in a sparsely furnished office on Broadway across from the Ed Sullivan Theater, once put it to me plainly: "How long have you known your mother didn't love you?"

I didn't know it then; I don't know that I know it now.

My mother never said "I love you." At the end of phone calls, and before long trips, I wouldn't say *love* either. None of us did; how could we?

As a family we never said "Good night," choosing instead to drift silently upstairs to our rooms and click our doors shut and read our books.

Like most mothers she would ask us when we were toddlers:

"Who loves you all the way up to the sky? Who loves you to the moon and back?" The answer had to be her.

Despite her beige home and beige clothes, she insisted that her favorite color was yellow—the color of anxiety; the color of the dented Volkswagen Rabbit she drove before Father bought our first station wagon. Her favorite song was "You Are My Sunshine," the lyrics—"please don't take my sunshine away"—revealing her terrible fear of what other mothers would consider growing up.

I would listen to her singing that Oirish self-parody, "Too-ra-loo-ra-loo-ral," to her youngest children, Sally and Tommy, in their bunk beds while I crouched in the hallway—"Hush now, baby, don't you cry"—and I'd find myself crying, mystified by a loneliness that felt like devastation. Where did it come from? What was wrong with me?

That royal mien babies possess, as if they expect you to cater to their every whim: I welcomed it with my daughter. Love is her due. But my mother was always accusing her children of "taking me for granted" and "taking advantage of me." She flummoxed us with this charge each time, because she had grown up with a butler and cooks and maids; she used to drive her father's Cadillac to high school, an embarrassment that pained her to remember. But her ungrateful children were "spoiled." So we resolved to ask even less of her.

Every September she took us to Epstein's Dry Goods in Tuckahoe for discount back-to-school clothes—stiff blue jeans, multipacks of briefs and tube socks—and the whole time I'd be choking back tears. Again, I didn't know why; I just knew I couldn't bear to owe her anything.

I felt safest when she needed me, felt flattered by her need—enlarged. She treated me as an equal, in these circumstances, or as an elder. I was her stand-in psychotherapist, certainly her confidant. We conspired like lovers. "You're very wise," she would say, and we'd change the subject or scatter as soon as we heard Father upstairs stirring.

When we fought I found I could go away from myself, like a patient in a dentist's chair. I'd will myself out of my body and make of my face a mask. All of her children possessed this ability; Paul's mask was hard and sharp and chilling to see. We knew we couldn't win an argument with her, because when she sensed she was losing she would turn to Father and betray us to his wrath.

But usually she just wanted me to listen. *How much is nature and how much is nurture?* She was forever asking herself, and me, this profound and profoundly unanswerable question, especially concerning Paul.

Why some people suffer more than others was an obsession she shared with me over and over again while asking my opinion about human behavior and motivation. But while she seemed to accept the medical definition of depression, she denied that psychotherapy had value. The stigma of diagnosis and treatment was far worse for a child than any so-called symptoms—that was her rationalization. But I knew she was afraid.

Probably she didn't love us because her parents didn't love her. Neglect was the recurring theme of the childhood memoir she never wrote. She'd been "dumped" at that sleepaway camp in Vermont when she was six. There weren't enough standby seats for everybody at Thanksgiving or Christmas, so her parents left her and her sisters at Idlewild with money for a taxi, while they jetted off to Florida or the Caribbean or wherever. And her mother left mentally when she drank, her father physically when he worked; neither of them were ever truly home. No wonder as a mother she hardly ever went out. No wonder she wanted us to stay at home with her.

When did my mother's speech first strike me as crazy? Surely it was long before I learned the meaning of the word *logorrhea*. Talk obfuscates as often as it explicates or implicates—more often; I learned this from her.

From her I learned also to talk ceaselessly, though I did so in my head. Hunkered in the bath I found myself conducting open-ended dialogues with myself, as if virtuosically sustaining every conversation in my mind's ear concerning anything, really, words and phrases bouncing in an endless volley, batting and battling to and fro—something like hearing voices, though her voice has always been strongest, effortlessly present. I can hear her voice now, though she is fading.

As we all know, or think we know, a mother's love for her child cannot be surpassed. But it's the child, lacking power and knowledge of the world, that clings to their mother with the more desperate passion. My love for my mother was total and nearly selfless—"nearly" because I knew I had to leave her. Following her from room to room I would ask, "Can I go to the bathroom?" Or, "Is it all right if I go up to my room to read?" Or, "I'm going outside to play. Is that okay?" As if my mother couldn't survive five minutes without me.

Sometimes she answered breezily that, yes, it was okay—of course!—that I go; yet I would feel compelled to confirm: "Are you sure?" And she would chuckle, saying, "Danny, why don't you ever believe what I say?"

Suburban Pastoral

LONG HAVE I longed to sing my celebration of gray and black squirrels. Crows in dogwoods, dogs on leashes, gypsy moth caterpillars oozing green blood. Bloodsucker worms in asphalt after rain; steam rising from the asphalt with the electric tang of ozone. The off-kilter chiming melodies of Good Humor and knife-sharpeners' trucks. Commuting fathers walking toward the station and returning at close of day in black woolen coats and silk burgundy scarves, swinging their briefcases like lunchboxes. Like boys on their way home from school.

Our road was Tunstall Road. Mother said the historical Tunstall had been English and a lord, but it was a mouthful to say. Mail often arrived addressed to "Turnstile." In person and over the phone we had to spell it.

I wish to preserve my childhood's locutions: "Sunday driver," "This is the pits," "D.O." (for "do over," but also, disconcertingly, my initials), "knuckle sandwich," "bum rap," "the booby hatch." When rain fell despite sunshine we would proclaim, "A monkey's getting married!" Do kids still talk this way?

Mother would send us next door for a cup of sugar or flour, a stick of butter; only later we learned how our neighbors resented these requests. This wasn't the 1950s. They'd been complaining to their children, who told us and we told her.

At Christmastime we'd ring their doorbells with homemade cookies warm on paper plates, wrapped in cling film and tied with red-and-green ringleted ribbons.

We'd wade a winding path through the Mormons' pachysandra to observe the Fitzgeralds' rabbits in their wire hutches; uncanny red-eyed familiars with teeth like horrid fingernails, their fecal pellets defacing last week's *Reporter Dispatch*. The Fitzgeralds were already old, their children in high school or college and their house therefore half empty. Clear plastic encased their living room furniture, dressed up with fusty afghans. Mr. Fitzgerald teetered atop his high ladder, painting old trim. Their tomboyish daughter Louise babysat us; in front of my family, as Mother peeled off a few bills, I asked, "Is Louise a boy or girl?" Their son Declan, lead singer of the high school band the Shattered Window Pains, played his Kiss records for me as we sat upon the mango shag in his bedroom. Square-jawed, unibrowed Ed Jr. acted off-off-Broadway—"He's a waiter," my mother would clarify.

The old neighbors haunted our dead end. Old women who kept their blinds drawn and forswore their front doors. Some of them were hoarders. A concrete Virgin Mary moldered in the bog of a backyard corner; cars from the '60s collected pollen, rust, bird droppings. Shrubs grew high into trees that bent low. The old neighbors had known the family that lived in our house before us, and the family before. The old neighbors were lonely. On holidays we watched from our bikes as adult children dragged themselves from their cars toward the front doors of their original dramas.

Mrs. Wallace was reclusive and obese and—when we caught sight of her—dressed in flowery muumuus. She kept a legion of cats. We rained pinecones and pebbles down upon her roof one summer twilight for no reason other than sheer boredom; she called our mothers to complain. Old Widow Abraham's colonial house was painted army green, and every so often she'd perform her civic duty by opening her doors for school classes to browse her moth-bitten midcentury memorabilia: postage stamps and presidential pins behind glass in a living room that looked more like a small-town museum. Weekends I'd help clean out the Careys' garage or attic or basement, their fluffy Shih Tzu yapping after us, for a wage of instant lemonade and a plate of butter cookies from the blue tin. Mr. Carey was a retired Manhattan copywriter, his son Dan was a fireman, and his other son Alan a painter who gave me free lessons before expatriating himself to Rome. The Rosenbaums retired to Florida so that their only son, a nebbishy computer animator, could move back home from the city with his cowgirl-booted, redheaded wife, rumored to have been an exotic dancer, and their eccentric toddler named Cody (who complemented his mother nicely by wearing daily not only boots but a cowboy hat and plastic six-shooter in his leather gun belt). I was amazed that the Rosenbaums' son could bear to raise his family in the house where he'd been raised.

The new family across the street was big like ours and Irish, or Irish American, and had moved here from the Bronx, my father's fatherland (though he never took us anywhere near the Bronx). Saturday morning I ventured down their long black freshly paved drive, so unlike our dusty stretch of weeds and gravel, and heard a voice speak from behind the sun: "How old are you?"

"Five."

"I'm six," he said, descending from the eyrie of his back

porch. We looked each over in the heat that radiated from the ticking hood of his father's magisterial black Cadillac.

Liam Sullivan was a freckly ginger, pudgy and precocious and sarcastic, apt to greet even the shyest boast with a derisory "Good for you!" His father was a barrel-chested, cigar-smoking bulldog who spent his days barking stock trades from the floor of 11 Wall Street. Mr. Sullivan's cigar smoke was pervasive; riding in the back of his Cadillac to a Yankees game was a nauseating ordeal. His wife chain-smoked Virginia Slims, and his children smoked everything—even Liam was puffing in the bushes by the time he was twelve. They were Catholic; Liam wore a maroon-and-gold cardigan, a white dress shirt and clip-on maroon tie, and gray wool slacks every weekday to the school bus at the top of our street, on his way to Iona Prep in New Rochelle. Patchily bearded Ben, one of Liam's two older brothers, warred with their mother and sulked in his attic bedroom, spinning Rolling Stones and Bowie records; the other brother, Carl, went missing for a week before he was found sleeping overnight in the high school gym's locker room (he was shipped off to a military academy posthaste). Liam's two sisters drank Tab by the six-pack while watching cable TV pantsless on weekends, the tails of their father's old dress shirts barely covering their panties—a fashion that drove me to distraction. Polly was a bit butch and rowdy; Sara the lissome brunette was a secretarial student at Katharine Gibbs in Manhattan, and to my dismay dating a guy with mutton chops and a mullet and a van painted with a sunset, complete with a mattress in back. I saw her naked silhouette one night from my window as she unhooked her bra in front of her window, the sodium flare of the streetlight buzzing between us. Or I dreamed this.

The Sullivans were not classy. In her ankle-length fur coat Liam's mother resembled a bootlegger's wife. Mr. Sullivan's watermelon-colored polyester slacks matched his hypertensive face. When Liam's uncle sold liquor to an underaged kid at his bar on the Upper East Side, and the kid then strangled a girl in Central Park that night, the Sullivans were more concerned that Uncle Donny, or "Mad Dog" as he was known, might lose his liquor license, despite an abundance of police and government connections. The Sullivans were nothing if not vestigial Tammany Hall.

Liam was my first best friend, his family the first of many surrogates, and I saw a lot of life in their house across the street, like the neck braces screwed into the closet doors on either side of Mr. and Mrs. Sullivan's bed, with crowns above for securing their skulls in place. I glimpsed them both once, husband and wife, sitting there all trussed up and impeccably postured, smoking in silence, each with an ashtray resting upon the expanse of bedspread between them—a vision like a poem of middle age, and a warning of some kind.

I wish for my daughter a swamp like ours that stewed and bubbled at the bottom of our dead end, with its brook seeping behind a chipped and peeling whitewashed fence. The water a wickery slush in winter, a stinking sludge in summer when, after working in the sun with Father, we'd dump our grass clippings and shrub cuttings into the inlets cloaked in brambles. Father told us that our brook trickled all the way to the Hudson River (or the Hutchinson, I was never sure which) and onward to the Atlantic.

Intrepidly we'd ford the brook from root to rock to stump, traversing the swamp in our sopping canvas sneakers, scrambling up onto a road in New Rochelle, the town where we'd been born, Mother often reminded us (or in its hospital, at least).

The swamp was taboo, and to my young mind druidic,

puddled with oily, rainbowed mirrors to the netherworld. A receptacle of spirits. Unknown teens left beer cans and butts in the cinders of their midnight fires.

We good children could vanish—stepping off the asphalt of the turnaround, or sweeping across the manicured meadow of Liam's backyard past his mother's boxed raspberry plants, plucking berries as we passed, smearing our teeth black with their grit and sweetness. Down into the swamp through the netting of overhanging grapevines, we'd crush a pungent trail through the broad-leafed, shin-high skunk cabbage, burs sticking to our sleeves and cuffs, into the shade of a realm our parents could no longer visit. Like knights-errant or Merry Men we sought out sunspots for spotlights in which to pause and plan and play our endless day. With matches stolen from our mothers' kitchens we burned plastic trash to release its green flames. Or gathering sticks as swords, we'd fight our epic battles with each other and other, unseen forces. My brother Steven would join—he didn't have many friends of his own; lugging a veritable log, he'd volunteer to play Little John, encircled in a clearing, on nobody's side, swiping and lunging at his foes. Our afternoons concluded with bruised and scraped knuckles, streaming noses and livid bug bites, and Mother throwing open the front door to ring us home for dinner with her copper handbell, turning green.

Summer evenings we congregated beneath streetlamps amid clouds of mosquitos, watching Dougie Hornik flex his forearm or bicep until the mosquito sucking his blood would burst. We played the traditional games like Truth or Dare and Light as a Feather, Stiff as a Board. We Kicked the Can. Freckled Samuel Pinker liked to launch toads skyward with a tennis racket, and when there wasn't a racket at hand he'd stuff a firecracker down a toad's throat and light it and run and come back giggling for the pieces. One night Samuel sprinted in the dark into a thorny rosebush, and his mother came to cradle him home like a casualty of war, and none of us felt sorry. Perched atop our kitchen counter, I bit the dishcloth as my mother used a stovetop-sanitized pin to tease a sliver of street-glass out of my thumb. With a dishcloth wet with hot water and soap, she'd scrub the grime from my neck. I looked forward to bedtime, because that's when I was able to imagine Stacey Madigan from around the corner in my arms as I sank into my slumber.

Soon we discarded our swords for Lugers, Magnums, M16s and AK-47s and AR-15s from Liam Sullivan's ever-growing cache of toy firearms. We fought the Germans and the Japanese, the Koreans and the Vietcong, and of course those dirty red Soviet commies. When we got shot we were honor-bound to hit the dirt and count to ten, before resurrecting ourselves eagerly into flight and more fight. Snug in my sniper's nest I found, not for the last time, that I preferred to wait and watch.

Sometimes we let Pat Connolly play. His father was bald and wore thick glasses like my father; cornflakes stuck to his cheeks as he walked the family's black Lab, Bandit, around the turnaround. He was an executive at IBM, the absentminded corporate nerd our father aspired to be. Mrs. Connolly was gaunt and German and usually gardening. When Pat claimed descent from the Irish revolutionary James Connolly, I was wildly jealous. He could be a crybaby, so we confiscated his gun: "Now we're playing Manhunt," we decreed, "and you're it."

In warm weather we rode our bikes as a gang and guarded the intersection of Madison and Tunstall from the Barry Road Boys, and from the Catholic kids up Tunstall hill. Soon we were old enough to pedal to Eastchester and Bob's, the candy and Lotto and magazine depot on Post Road where, along with baseball cards and comic books, we'd purchase chewing-gum cigarettes. We blew the sugar out like smoke, then unwrapped and chewed the tasteless gum with tough-guy resolve.

Mrs. Friedman was diagnosed with multiple sclerosis, took up poetry, and was publishing obscurely; Mr. Friedman, clad in plaid pants or shorts, a proud multigenerational Dartmouth legacy, treated her often to off-Broadway theatre. ("Some of these plays are so strange, Danny," he confided in me from behind his sharp-edged box hedge, quizzically, as if I might be able to enlighten him.) Their son, a freshman at Dartmouth, spun me around their yard one late-summer night and let me go sailing into the stars of a mild concussion. My father said everybody who went to Dartmouth was "an asshole. They just can't help it."

Summers were ending, again and again. We withdrew into our houses, found friends in other parts of town. We went away to school. But the swamp, I like to believe, is still as it was.

"Good"

I CLUNG TO her thighs and knees, kicked at the jambs, arched my back and fell limp and contorted myself again, squawking and scratching at my mother's skin. "The poor boy," said the teachers, two matronly hippies in bell-bottomed denim, their gray-streaked ponytails unraveling as they struggled to disentangle me from my mother.

For weeks I refused to leave the cubby room, where coats hung on hooks above rainboots in square holes; and from my seclusion I observed Jordan Davis singing senselessly in his high girlish voice, kneeling backward in the lap of a turquoise chair, snipping construction paper carelessly in the air above his shimmery mop top. I wondered how anybody could feel so free.

The school smelled of paste and paint and Magic Markers, of the safety scissors' gummy rubber handles, of the sadness of last week's accidental urination or worse. I envied my classmates, though I never figured out what they were finding so exciting about school: things looked pointless from where I stood in the shadow of the cubby room.

Bossy, with a mischievous grin and an upturned nose dusted with freckles, Melissa was blond and blue-eyed and took pity on me. The trees outside the cubby room's basement windows shed their leaves, the sky was bruised; this would be my first Irish morning, as it were, my first conscious feeling of the refuge of inclemency. Melissa coaxed me out into the open, then immediately teased me: "Danny Diaper." I hurled the Lite-Brite at her patent leather shoes and frilly socks, scaring myself more than her with the detonation of those multicolored pegs across the linoleum tiles. But I never stayed in the cubby room again.

Melissa and I were friends after that. One afternoon in my attic on the black-and-white TV we were watching *Them*, a genre classic concerning carpenter ants made mutantly huge by atomic testing in New Mexico (the movie would infiltrate my nightmares for years), and Melissa needed to go potty. I came downstairs to see what was taking her so long, and from the toilet she swung open the door with her foot: "Want to watch, Danny Diaper?"

I declined; I was rattled. But already I had a type. I told my mother I intended to marry a blond girl with blue eyes and move to California, and at least this dream, I am amused to note, has been realized.

The neighborhood was called Edgewood because at some point in time there had been a wood where our quarter-acre homesteads now stood. Edgewood Elementary was built in 1918. Frances the crossing guard, in a straw-colored wig, a silver whistle bit between lipstick-stained teeth, held up her white-gloved hand (or was it a stop-sign paddle?) to shepherd us in our frolicsome clumps from the corner to the sidewalk beside the playing field. Then the reverse at three.

I walk through the school in my memories: the high antechamber to the principal's office flooding with drowsy sunlight; the open hallway closet, where teachers spun glumly the purple drum of the mimeograph machine; the oasis of a sickroom with its seafoam vinyl chaise, and the wide magnifying halo through which the school nurse's lunar face would peer while picking through our locks for lice; the thick newels of the staircase from the lower to the upper grades, where one afternoon in our climb an older boy trumpeted from above the news that the pope had been shot through the hand.

The honey-hued rosin cake encased in its block of sap-gum wood, rubbed along the fraying fibrous horsehair of our violin bows, unleashed a forest of perfume. For extra credit we clapped the chalk dust out of our teachers' black felt erasers. We ate our lunch meats smeared with yellow mustard on white bread in the stuffy zoo of the school's meeting room, foraging for sweets from the food-swap table. The sons and daughters of Japanese businessmen arrived in the mid-1980s with their seaweed paper and rice. The morning light toppled in columns across the cavern of the assembly hall that doubled as our gym, where we swayed dizzily atop metal bleachers at choral concerts while massacring, yet again, *Godspell*'s "Day by Day." Our librarian, Mrs. Golding, went away and came back without her breasts, or so we overheard (she looked the same to us; but altered irrevocably, we could tell). Our mothers sat on the low curving flagstone wall at three, rocking our younger siblings in strollers or carriages, waiting to walk us home.

Mrs. Balsam, my kindergarten teacher, possessed—in my innocent appraisal—a fetching figure. In her tight pencil skirts, creamy blouses, and lustrous high heels, she was an Eisenhower-era beauty with coal-black hair, ruby lipstick, and a convincing beauty mark. I'd position myself at the head of the line, directly behind Mrs. Balsam's behind as we marched through the hallway to music or art or gym class. She used the

Yiddish word *tuchus* when telling us to sit on our behinds. I asked my mother why my teacher's tuchus swayed "back and forth like that," and she fixed me in her gaze a moment before answering enigmatically: "That's just how some women are . . ."

One morning I planted a thumbtack, pin up, on the seat of Mrs. Balsam's chair. I didn't have a reason why. An hour or so later she announced to the class that she had, just a moment before, been grievously wounded, physically and psychologically, and there would be no recess until the culprit confessed and apologized. She had no wish to shame anybody, she said, so we were to line up and whisper our confession (or denial) in her ear. "It was somebody else," I heard myself hiss when my turn came. I was thrilled. We were let out to recess, where playground gossip confirmed that Richie Christopher, our most hyperactive classmate, had been the one to dishonestly confess, so distressing was the prospect of an entire day spent indoors for him.

Dowdy Mrs. Dupont in first grade plonked and pedaled at the upright piano, encouraging me to duet with her—"Daisy, Daisy / Give me your answer, do / I'm half crazy / All for the love of you"—but I was afraid of seeming girlish. In second grade Mrs. Asner, the hypochondriac, called me "chivalrous" for holding the door for her. In third grade I liked to tease Miss Smart—a pixie-haired young woman fond of an exotic new foodstuff called yogurt, and destined to marry Dr. Molloy, our principal (a doctor of what, we wondered? certainly not discipline)—with surreptitious farting sounds. Mrs. Fiderer told me that I had what it took to be a writer when I grew up. Our classroom served as a scholastic experiment of sorts; we spent every afternoon of fourth and fifth grade with Mrs. Fiderer, writing stories and poems at our desks, before bringing them to a round table in the corner by the ferns for the critique of our peers—hardly different from my experience years later in graduate school at Brown.

Some other characters worth noting: Mrs. Papadakis, a recurrent (and clueless) substitute teacher, with hair a pale magenta like the inside of a conch; our school janitors in their gray jumpsuits, suave Silvio with the sideburns and white-haired Ray, who'd throw his Donald Duck impression like a ventriloquist behind us in the hallway as we passed; and my final teacher at Edgewood, Miss Petty, tall and elderly and birdlike, if a vulture should be considered a bird, who lost her patience one morning and condemned us all to lives of hard labor as "garbagemen" (and -women, one presumes). Miss Petty rolled her eyes when she learned I had won second prize in a nationwide short story contest in *Cricket Magazine* ("the *New Yorker* for Children," according to its founding editor). She was by no means the last teacher to resent my artistic aspirations.

One memory stands out from these years, regarding my writing. In third grade Miss Smart asked me to read my story to the class. She was so impressed that she brought me around to other classrooms, other grades, interrupting their day to have me read to them too. "Isn't he *good*?" she asked.

My IQ was nothing to write home about, my mother told me many times, certainly nowhere near as impressive a score as hers which, again, qualified her as a genius, at least technically speaking. None of her children could quite reach her level, although I'd apparently tested the lowest to date. She never told me the exact number; she didn't want to inhibit me in any way, she said.

She could have been lying—about her score and mine. I won prizes, trophies, ribbons, and she never seemed to care. If another mother spoke favorably of my talents, she would smile slightly, almost mockingly and say "Oh? You think so?" Her excuse was that she didn't want any child of hers to suffer from a "swelled head."

When we brought home our report cards—good grades because Mother said they had to be, and anyway it felt good to be good at something—she'd send us into the living room, where we'd wait patiently for a commercial break before presenting Father with our slips of paper. "Better than I ever did," was all he ever said after an irritated glance, before handing the slip back as if he'd punched a train ticket.

An older boy wanted to fight me for no reason. He bashed my nose; I tackled him and ground his cheek into the cement. He never bothered me again.

I must have bullied. I don't recall orchestrating the torment—that was typically Kevin Hurley, whose father, a US Marine vet and a cop, slapped his son in public for any and all misdemeanors—but I fear I kept silent in the presence of abuse.

There were too many Dannys in my classes: Danny D, Danny J, Danny W. I was Danny O and my friends were Neil Matthews, Jordan Davis, Rich Christopher, Tim Bryant; we were known as the boys with first names for last names (more or less). We had been friends since nursery school, owing mainly to inertia.

Tim had devilish eyes in a dimpled, cherubic face. Pleasantly bothersome, he was the friend we made fun of. We swiped his prized Yankees cap from his head and tossed it over and around him on the way home from school. We slugged his arm if we spied a VW Bug drive past. I knew we were wrong; but why did he have to be so annoying? Surely he was capable of more self-control. Couldn't he, like me, at least try to deny and defy who he was?

Tim's house was a mess. His father drove a run-down Subaru we called the Snot Mobile because it was green and sticky, with dog hair everywhere and dog saliva coating the windshield which their Jack Russell licked for the coolness and condensation. Buddy was the dog's name, and regularly he went around collared in a cone of shame due to one infection or another. Tim called his father Wilbur and his mother Sue. Wilbur called "Soo-ie!" across the house to his sturdy and unfussy wife, as if summoning the hogs to feed. Our father referred to Wilbur as a "bleeding-heart liberal," and I did once witness Mr. Bryant conversing compassionately with a bag lady outside the movie theater on Garth Road. He was forever campaigning for some local or regional office, and winning too. He took credit for passing New York State's first bottle redemption bill. He corrected our grammar every chance he got. Thick hairs sprouted from his ear canals and pendulous lobes and the tip of his fleshy nose (his antennae-like "feelers," he would joke). A rug on his side of the bed—embroidered in an earlier age by an old flame—read, as if a pearl of folksy wisdom: "Wilbur Bryant Is Hot Shit." That love affair ended because of his drinking, according to his son, but he was sober now, perpetually walking his little Buddy up and down our neighborhood streets as if trying to outpace his thirst.

In the fall the Bryants would drive Tim and his friends to their country house upstate, a ramshackle cottage haunted by a mid-century dentist's chair that had been bolted to the living room floor, an artifact of the previous owner's occupation. Pubic hairs littered the misaligned toilet seat and pee-splattered tiles of the house's only bathroom. We boys liked to stay up late telling jokes and reading Tolkien in Tim's room, which had been a porch, curled up against a wall of rusty-hinged windows that looked in upon a living room where the evening's fire was

collapsing into embers. I found it funny, and strangely insulting, that the Bryants called their closest upstate neighbors the
"Crazy O'Briens," for—among other reasons—nightly setting
loose their pack of barking mutts in the woods surrounding.

My parents visited once. As we walked with the Bryants
along rural train tracks through a conflagration of foliage, Tim
discovered that he enjoyed the feeling of ramming his head into
my father's crotch repeatedly, despite Father's tepid dissuasions.
"It's just a phase," said Wilbur, and everybody laughed, except
Father whose impotent rage in these moments was a delight
to behold.

Back in Scarsdale a blizzard blew in during Tim's confirma-
tion party, and he climbed onto the roof outside his bedroom
window to read. Nobody knew why he'd done this; to com-
mune with nature? We locked him out there for an hour or
so, as the snow accrued on his head, shoulders, knees, loafers.
He kept on reading his Vonnegut, or Stephen King. Months
earlier we'd caught him crying on Neil Matthew's bed as he
pored through a *Newsweek* cover story about global warming
("Danger: More Hot Summers Ahead"). It was his self-righ-
teous conscientiousness that seemed to justify—no, to necessi-
tate—our decision to record an audio mockumentary entitled
Tim Bryant: Portrait of a Loser and provide him with a copy.

Our world was white, with the exception of a Chinese girl
who'd been adopted by Irish American parents after their
daughter drowned in a backyard pool. And those Japanese
businessmen, with their smiling wives and non-English-speak-
ing children. A car salesman remarked to my mother in my
presence that I was, like him, "black Irish," which confused me
because I was so pale.

Some of the garbagemen in town were Black; we'd see them

in the street hanging off the back of the garbage trucks, or through the kitchen window as they shook the contents of our cans into their trolleys, then rolled the trolleys back out to the street to dump our trash into the truck's fetid, crushing maw.

I had a Black teacher in fourth grade, and by high school two Black classmates (one of whom happened to be this teacher's son). We watched Martin Luther King's "I Have a Dream" on the TV in the school library. As a Current Event we discussed Bernie Goetz's shooting of Black teenagers in the subway. In high school I sat on my bed and watched live on my sister's old black-and-white set the riots in Los Angeles. I remember vividly the white man pulled from the cab of his truck to be brained by a Black man with a brick.

One rainy afternoon on our way to the Galleria Mall in White Plains my brother and I were rear-ended. Steven was driving our family's new used car, the powder-blue Buick Regal with the matching blue velveteen interior bought for a pittance from the Sawyers, the Mormons next door.

The accident occurred in front of Grace Church at four in the afternoon, when the sidewalk was crowded with Black men. The driver who hit us was Black, his car skidding on the wet asphalt; in the mirror I saw him reach behind his ear nonchalantly for a pen. But the men in the street around us were shouting. John Lennon's "Woman" was playing on our radio.

A Black man swung himself into our back seat. "There's going to be a riot," he said. He slammed the door. "Drive!"

I thought we were about to be robbed. The rain was relentless. He needed a ride to the hospital, he said; his arm had been broken "by crackheads" in a beating at the shelter and hadn't healed right. He wanted me to see. "Go on," he said, "touch," holding out his forearm to display the bump where the bone tented his skin. As my brother drove I reached into the back seat and touched it.

He changed his mind: money would be more helpful than the hospital. What did we have? He took what we gave him and stepped into the street at the next light.

Was I a good boy? I believed I was, or tried to be. I saw myself as basically fair and carried myself with a noblesse oblige that grown-ups mischaracterized as maturity.

Undeniably I had my faults. Sheltered, or sequestered, I was racist by osmosis; homophobic and sexist too. I was cruel to Tim Bryant and others because I was afraid of them—of being or becoming them—just as I was afraid of my siblings, who, for all their good manners, were awkward and lonely and bad at being kids. I was most frightened of any resemblance to my brother Paul, whose creeping depression I misunderstood as laziness and cowardice.

I decided—I don't know when—that as Paul and my other siblings failed, I would succeed. As they were spurned, I would win love. As they were rejected and ignored, I would garner applause. I would be good. And when I ended up failing, as I could not fail to, I would suffer with a wretchedness that felt familiar, like how I imagined they felt, and I would catch an inkling of the realization that we were more than similar: we were facets of the same abused child. The pressure to be otherwise was too much.

Symptoms

SLEEPWALKING RAN IN the family, so to speak. My mother's baby sister Darcy sleepwalked through the worst of their family's turmoil, wandering the dark halls of Auld Ridge with her eyes open, eerily unseeing. And in the morning remembered nothing.

My mother would find me trudging up and down stairs, pissing in the bathroom hamper, lurking in her doorway like a golem.

"What are you doing, Danny?"

"Watching."

Or "I'm going downstairs."

Or "What does it look like I'm doing? I'm pissing."

She'd say "affronted" was my attitude, as I sleepwalked myself back to bed. It could make her laugh.

Many mornings I woke up with my face flat against the sheets. My pillow had gone missing in the night; I would find it stuffed on a basement shelf, or behind a ladder in the garage, or in the kitchen closet where, as a younger boy, I had liked to hide and observe my family through the crack in the door. It was unsettling, and impressive—the agency of my unconscious mind, this secret self who was apparently capable of doing whatever he wanted, whatever that was.

Like all children I saw ghosts. They looked bored. Late at night a woman with a babushka's headscarf materialized, seated on an invisible chair, squeezing a soundless accordion. An old man dressed like a station agent leaned against my brother Steven's dresser, examining a silver pocket watch.

Faces coalesced in the leaves and needles of the trees outside my window. Orbs bounced along the ceiling. I slept with my blanket wrapped around my neck through the hottest summer nights, to protect against vampires. The throb of my heartbeat upset me, so I slept on my right side with my face pressed close to the edge of the mattress, so I wouldn't be surprised by the rising visage of a zombie or gray space alien.

Mr. Carey walked his Shih Tzu to the turnaround and back at night. I would hear his scuffling limp—but when I'd pull back the curtain: only the empty street below, lit by the glow of the streetlamp that seemed to grow out of our unkempt privet hedge.

Light, as every child knows, is antiseptic to ghosts and monsters. So I'd crack my curtain to let the street- and moonlight in, and from my pillow I'd watch and wait for sleep. On winter nights, hoping school might be cancelled in the morning, I checked and rechecked our streetlamp's cone of amber for the first falling flakes of tomorrow's reprieve.

From our front hallway the tick-tock and chimes of a wall clock, like the head and chest only of a grandfather clock, measured my loneliness through the night. When the clock fell silent it stayed that way for days or weeks; until Father inserted the key in the clock face and cranked, cranked, cranked . . . Then he'd set the pendulum in motion again.

Ghosts were common but death was not. Milly was the

youngest Sawyer; with straight brown hair and long, lean, tanned thighs, she cradled her lacrosse ball in her lacrosse stick expertly in her front yard next to ours. Until one evening our doorbell rang: "I hate to be the bear of bad tidings"—I thought I heard the strange man say "bear" (strangeness within strangeness)—"but Milly Sawyer has died." A car crash, he said. On her way home from Brigham Young at the end of her freshman year with two of her friends, driving day and night, and during her shift at the wheel Milly fell asleep. The car careened off the interstate in the dawn light of Nebraska. Nobody was wearing seatbelts and the car rolled four times. Her friends, two young men, walked away practically unscathed: an injured wrist, some stitches. Giddily—and guiltily—I raced upstairs to tell the rest of my family the news.

That afternoon from the Peery's driveway, the neighborhood kids watched the visitors arrive: dressed in black, bearing plates of covered food; we found it odd, certainly beyond our comprehension, that a party could be so quiet. Mrs. Sawyer left the house with her husband helping her navigate the front walk to their car, both of them invalided overnight by their grief. We tossed gravel into the street. Days later I accompanied my mother to Milly's memorial service because my father had declined to go.

When the Sawyers would vacation, in Hawaii or out west with family, I fed and walked their poodle Shem. Like his Biblical namesake, one of Noah's sons and the eponymous primogenitor of the "Shemitic" or Semitic tribes, this canine Shem was Methuselean and palpably tumor-stricken. He'd been Milly's puppy. Unlocking their front door and stepping inside, I felt like a grave robber. Only Milly's framed high school graduation portrait adorned the top of their polished black grand piano. Lamps on timers snapped on and off; stereo speakers blasted to life with Mormon hymns. I'd dole out some kibble, fill Shem's bowl with water; then search the house, beneath Ned and Holly's bed, then the other bedrooms and upstairs to the attic and the dead girl's room where I might hear Shem's tinkling tags, and see my light flashing in his cataract-clouded eyes under her bed.

I'd pull him out gently and leash him, lead him down step by step; or carry him outside when he was shaking, and stand him up in the grass. He'd pee on my leg if I wasn't careful. Then back inside. I'd slam the door on my way out again—desperate to get home to my familiar ghosts.

The book was entitled *Symptoms* and lived in the bookcase behind a potted plant at the rear of our living room, alongside our hundredfold *National Geographic* magazines, my father's *Jonathan Livingston Seagull*, Carlos Castaneda, and a Time-Life history of Nazi Germany that contained one particularly shocking photo of a girl laughing as a brownshirt pulled up her skirts, his long knife held, blade down, above her bush.

Symptoms was a home medical guide intended as a revolution in pragmatism. One looked for one's symptoms in an index up front, then proceeded to the indicated page where one would be reliably provided with the worst diagnosis imaginable.

I was forever poking around my neck and jawline for swollen glands. When my mother was overwhelmed by my hypochondria she would bring me to Father. Paul had pegged me in the eye with a wild grape from the swamp; surely I was going blind. I was coming down with AIDS, acquired by accidentally brushing against the posterior of an effeminate man in the bookstore. I had cancer, etc.

"You'll never hear the bullet that kills you" was my father's only advice, like something he'd heard John Wayne growl in a foxhole in a movie long ago. And with that our consultation was concluded.

But he was a hypochondriac too, of course. When he and Mother had trouble settling on a name for Tommy (he was their sixth child; the Mistake, the Gift from God), she suggested "Colin" but Father refused because, what with his nervous digestion, he suspected his colon was the organ that would kill him. And every few months he'd spend the day in bed: "Stress," Mother would explain, or "His stomach." He never acknowledged any weakness of any kind within earshot of his children. Despite his worry, though, he distrusted doctors. He was afraid of them—afraid of paying too. We went without health insurance and received our yearly checkups at school. Whatever the symptom, his response was to ignore it and hope it would go away.

She lifted me to the running faucet and propped me against the sink. She scooped the soap out of the dish and rolled its slickness into foam, scoured with her nails my knuckles and fingers and palms, then rinsed us both in the scalding water: clean.

She knelt before me. This wasn't religion, this was a strategy. Had I done the thing I was not supposed to do? I don't recall what. Forking my dinner beneath the kitchen window screen again; or had that been Steven? I lied, naturally. Lying seemed the only thing to do—morally correct, in a way—provided I could convince her. One must believe one's own lie first, I knew already. "I believe you, Danny," she lied. "But God knows the truth. And He will not forgive you, unless you confess and apologize." I did not say a word.

The cover of the book on the floor of my room read *The Prince of Life*. (Where had it come from?) Here was the true story, its subtitle promised rather enigmatically, of "the Son of Man."

I asked her: "If Jesus is the son of Man and also the son of God—does that mean Man is God?"

She didn't have an answer for that.

I told her I'd solved the mystery of the cross: the shorter, horizontal line represented life on earth, and the vertical ascending or descending suggested our eternal destinations. "My son"—she smiled—"the poet."

A psychotherapist would say I concocted a heavenly Father because I lacked a terrestrial one; or I had a father I didn't want; or I would want him if only he would want me. The Old Testament fathered me, then; or better yet I would beget myself, in time. I had a Jesus complex regardless. Or alternatively I would be David, or Jeremiah, in His honor composing my psalms and jeremiads, the prolific juvenilia of the prodigy. I longed to hear His small, still voice calling my name in the middle of my long, sleep-wrecked nights.

Or was I Joseph? The youngest of Israel, the comely son who wore his mother Rachel's bridal coat and dreamed of his own wisdom until lo, his jealous brothers dumped him down a well. I admired Joseph's tenacity, and the weepy, overly complicated revenge he carried out decades later against his brothers in Egypt. I wished without knowing it for a fatherly love like that which he ultimately received: "Now let me die, since I have seen thy face," said Jacob, reconciled with his son at last, "because thou art yet alive."

As I walked home from school, the windblown leaves in the laurel trees seemed to ring pantheistically like bells, like tongues in the mouths of bells, like angels singing a song beyond song; joy was felt, if fleetingly perceived. God's companionship was dependable in those years. Just over and behind my ear I heard Him.

I tried my best to proselytize to my younger sister Sally,

arranging her beside me on my bedspread and reading aloud some child-friendly passages from Genesis. Wearing her pink-and-purple sweat suit, she shook her copper curls and yawned, unbelieving or simply unentertained.

The book of Daniel I took personally, praying thrice daily as the prophet extolled. Morning and evening was easiest, in bed. Lunch was trickier; I'd abscond to my room on weekends, or into a chain link corner of the schoolyard. With practice I grew adept at praying without moving my lips in rote run-on sentences spooling out speaking in my mind thank you for everything I have and forgive me for everything I have done and everything I have yet to do but forgive me please God O forgive me most of all for my many sinful thoughts. I had read in the Bible that thinking of sin was as sinful as sinning, and thinking seemed ceaseless so praying ought to be too.

In Sunday school a pair of beautiful blond newlyweds passed around a postcard for each of us of the books of the Old and New Testaments, depicted in pen and ink like the spines of real, discreet volumes on the shelves of a bookcase. At home I propped the card on my night table; if it flittered to the floor, as often happened when I was making my bed, and my sheet or blanket or bedspread kicked up a draft, I'd have to immediately restore my totem to its altar and fall to my knees to pray, again, for forgiveness. In retrospect a God with such stringent yet arbitrary rules wasn't much of an improvement on my father, and in many ways His omniscience made Him worse. But if He was punishing me with my piety then I hadn't noticed yet.

My obsessive-compulsive disorder, when I understood what it was, spoiled organized religion for me; any service I attended, no matter the faith, looked like OCD en masse. Not that I blamed anybody. To suffer together seemed to be the point of religion, and perhaps this purpose was holy enough.

My mother had been raised Episcopal, a compromise between her mother's Lutheranism and her father's Methodism (or was it the other way around?) but also as a bid upward in the social strata—Episcopalians were the moneyed class, after all. She had long ago soured on St. James the Less in Scarsdale (too drearily medieval) where she'd gone as a girl, and over time we sampled the local Congregationalists, the Friends, and the aforementioned Mormons. We lasted longest at St. John's in Larchmont. To arrive in time for morning prayer at this Episcopal church by the sea required a journey out of Scarsdale past her old mansion, Auld Ridge, on the corner of Griffen and Weaver, and it was on these drives that I first heard many of the doleful tales of my mother's childhood.

St. John's was supposed to look English and Gothic. Its cornerstone read 1894. Armored in my Sunday best, blue blazer with brass anchor buttons, tight white collar with clip-on tie, gray wool slacks and thin black socks, I felt safe at St. John's, alone with my thoughts but together with a congregation of strangers, sitting and kneeling and standing, reciting and singing (though nobody in my family sang; I would at least mouth the words) beneath looming windows of stained glass. The wooden beams of the ceiling looked like the inside of an upturned Viking longship. The air smelled of graveyards and incense, coffee and Clorox and crayons. Only the Peace gave me pause—all those hand germs. Surprisingly I wasn't scared to share the communion cup, considering there was only a symbolic napkin wipe between each communicant's lips. I trusted that some form of spiritual disinfectant was at play here.

Outside and across the paved drive in Fountain Square there was fittingly a fountain: a bronze sculpture of a topless, muscular double-tailed mermaid, playing her double pipe to lull a stolen child to sleep. Water gurgled around and over these mossy figures into a circular basin bobbing with lily pads. An old folks' home nearby lent a poignancy to the neighborhood, with its broad porch populated by the elderly who sat rocking, blankets on their laps, looking out toward the sailboats on the surface of the Sound.

One Easter morning before church I felt an unbounded relief at the self-evident reality of the Resurrection. Sunlight danced in the gauze curtains of our living room. How I grieved as, within seconds, my revelation of grace dissipated with the arrival of clouds in the sky.

We went to church without Father. My older brothers were confirmed at St. John's, but after Paul's suicide attempt our attendance dwindled to just me and Mother, and I'd have to ask her to take me. She turned against that church too: they were hypocrites and snobs, she said, who'd shake your hand while saying the Peace then cut you off in their luxury cars while exiting the parking lot afterward—"Late for brunch at the yacht club again," she'd say. When I was fourteen I declined to be confirmed, and nobody cared. By then I had discovered another passion.

"Teenage Love"

WE FOUND IT in the rocks at school, wrinkled and waterlogged with rain. A Rudolph Valentino lookalike, wearing a kaffiyeh and absolutely nothing else, was preparing to penetrate a pouting Clara Bow type. A naked couple achieved shallow intercourse while swinging from a flying trapeze. We spirited our contraband home and stashed it in Mr. Britain's woodpile. But the next day the hole was vacant. Pretty Mrs. Britain, who'd been a stewardess with Pan-Am, confronted us: she was calling our mothers, she said. But she never did. Maybe her husband intervened.

Luckily I'd already torn a page free: a woman with frizzed black hair like my mother's, sitting astride a gleaming Harley-Davidson, unclothed save for a studded black leather jacket. I jammed the page into my pocket—I had to have it with me, had to keep it hidden behind the desk in my bedroom, then between the wall and my mattress.

Peter Coyle's mother was a child psychologist who, to our amazement, gave her son a subscription to *Playboy* as a gift on his thirteenth birthday. She didn't want him to feel ashamed, Peter explained. Why couldn't we have mothers like her?

Tony Barone knew he wanted to work as a laborer, for Con

Ed or the Metro-North rail. He'd often brag at school that he could peruse, whenever he wished, his father's extensive collection of dirty magazines. So one day I came over to play. My brother Steven was home sick in bed, and I suggested to Tony that a *Playboy* would surely improve Steven's health. Could I borrow just one issue? Tony agreed, but on the condition that I help construct a birthday gift for his mother out of scraps of two-by-fours and salvaged nails. In the basement we hammered the winter afternoon away. We were building a warship for his mother. As I was leaving Mrs. Barone bent down to zip my coat: "What's this?" she said, smiling as she extricated the magazine from beneath my shirt. My mother stood inside their front door looking mortified. Father was waiting in the car. "You know, Hugh Hefner is a very smart man," was all he said as we drove away.

My mother bought our dress clothes at the County Boys and Mens Shop downtown. We'd rent the tuxedoes for our prom here soon. But the measuring started young.

Two men, one white-haired, mantislike, the other a portly redhead, insisted on close fittings. They'd speak to each other in hushed tones, as they placed the boy atop a platform inside their three-way mirror at the back of the shop. I found it hair-raising when the redheaded one knelt to measure my inseam. He pressed the tape inside my ankle, then inched up my calf, knee, thigh, into my crotch—brief, but a touch, palpably a touch—while the wintry mantis watched, rubbing his hands together at the glass counter. Still—easier than a doctor's visit.

One evening over dinner my father shared the common knowledge with his children that the County Boys and Mens Shop was run by two men who were "light in the loafers." He didn't seem outraged or disgusted. "Men like that are good dressers."

We were playing Wiffle ball in Adam Caruso's corner yard, where the traffic at twilight was unabated. "God gives fags cancer!" he was shouting, waving his plastic bat. "God gives fags cancer!" as if joking. His parents, we'd learned, were divorcing (I'd found him crying in the coatroom at lunch and he told me). My aunt Gwendolyn's friend's husband was dying of AIDS in Greenwich; he'd been secretly gay. My sister's Math teacher went on leave and died of AIDS. My Spanish teacher Señor Kaminsky wove references to "Señora Kaminsky" into his classroom presentations, though the students knew without knowing that Señora Kaminsky did not exist. An English teacher, who seemed to like my short stories, was rumored to live tempestuously with both a man and a woman—an arrangement I found both baffling and terribly frightening.

My nipples swelled, puffy and pink. I felt them weeping, but when I checked I'd find them dry.

Mother chaperoned as Dr. Linden fondled me. His nails were jagged (he was a nervous nail-biter, Mother explained) and dandruff dusted the shoulders of his old tweed. He smiled queerly. Gynecomastia was his diagnosis, a mild case. My hormones, and with them my breasts, would level out in time.

I wore oversize T-shirts and worried I was metamorphosing into a third sex, like Tiresias (I'd read *Antigone* in school and suspected already that I, too, was a kind of a seer). I prayed that Mother would not tell Father.

"Look out for men holding hands," he said. He fell quiet as he drove while we tittered in back. And sure enough we did spot men holding hands, some swinging purses.

In the art supply store a woman in a denim skirt with hair like dune grass handed me the watercolors. She'd been working with her mother here since she was a girl. Through the windows I saw gaunt men with raspberry lesions rolling by on beach cruisers. The dry ovals of paint rattled in the cool metal case. "Danny is the artist of the family," my mother informed the woman, whose leathery hands, I realized now, were enormous, powerful.

On our way out of Provincetown our father spoke with just the slightest shiver of titillation: "Could you tell? That woman who helped us was really a man!"

We ducked between the rhododendrons and the stucco of Liam Sullivan's house. The game was his idea; he called it "Teenage Love," though we weren't teens yet. He gathered the warm cushions from the sun chairs on his porch, and tossed them onto the shaded earth and roots.

Liam's family had cable, so he'd seen R-rated movies. He snorted when I answered that yes, I knew what a dick was: "An enormous whale," I said, impressively because I'd yet to read Melville's classic. And essentially we'd just hold each other, Liam and I, face to shoulder; we never kissed. He smelled of cigarettes and butter-fried ham. We were erect, painfully tight against our zippers. Was I aware of his hardness, or only my own? Was he the girl or was I? He was older than me by a year and three days.

I knew this was pretend, a rehearsal. I would have rather been embracing Stacey Madigan from around the corner, hearing her voice whisper words like "harder" and "deeper" instead of his.

While Mr. Peery dripped sweat into the blades of his manual mower, kneeling in his skimpy track shorts to oil the gears, and Liam's father smoked his cigar through the window just above us, we clung to each other in silence, our hearts beating like rabbits.

My father never discovered us (nobody did, as far as I knew). "Teenage Love" ended—after how many weeks or months I can't recall—when Liam invited another boy to play with us; in the shade of the driveway beneath the Sullivan porch, the boy's response was repugnance, then an ambiguous disappointment: "My mother wouldn't like it." Liam moved away soon after, and later I heard he'd joined the Navy.

When I remembered "Teenage Love," especially as a teenager, I'd flush with shame and feel queasy: I had done something that could never be erased. I had to repress it—had to forget it, if I could. This was a secret I would take to my grave, as Mother said of the raccoons we'd buried, as she would say after my brother's suicide attempt.

Behind the radiator in the bathroom one night I found a tattered paperback that held the aura of a sacred text. The pages were pulpy and yellowing; the words were sex tips: "Insert the testicle in your mouth and suckle it gently like a robin's egg." I went to the bathroom many times that night, as intrigued by what the book had to say as by the mystery of who it was that had hidden it there. By the morning it was gone.

I did it all over the house—once after finishing *Tess of the d'Urbervilles* for Honors English. Steven's *Sports Illustrated* swimsuit issues heightened the thrill, as did the lingerie catalogs Father brought home from one of his few clients, Lejaby in White Plains. My mother's *Redbook* and *Ladies' Home Journal* could get the job done in a pinch. Then one day I discovered, hardback in brown cloth, *The Joy of Sex* and *More Joy of Sex* in Father's closet. I dared not think about my parents reading it, or committing any of the acts so graphically described and depicted therein, but the risk was worth it. I'd sneak into their bedroom whenever I could to scrutinize these books, though the creaturely hair repulsed me, and the male model was a dead ringer for Charles Manson.

There was a man in the Scarsdale Plaza, the hilltop art deco movie theater on Garth Road with the gluey cement floor, the stained and pilled velvet seats. Stale popcorn, liquid butter, the smell of urine cakes from the men's room. This was a Saturday matinee: just a man, my friend, and me.

At first I wasn't sure: Was he a wizened old woman? He turned around and stared at us. His face looked burned, his scarf like a bandage. His fedora tilted, wilted. He rose up the aisle as if levitating, then sat precisely in front of us in the next row. I whispered to my friend that we should leave.

The man made noises with his mouth: flatulent, excretory. Was he trying to befriend us? He turned and crouched and pressed his face between the seats. His feline eyes glistened. His skeletal hand unfolded before our faces, pointing up at the projector's swirl of colored light.

That night I couldn't sleep. The wind stripped the buds from the branches of our dogwood tree. I came to Mother and she listened to my fear: "That man is out there now."

Opposite of Me

SHE SENDS ME to fetch him for dinner and climbing the stairs I see him hanging from a noose. In my mind's eye. His feet are dancing inches off the floor; his slight body sways, twists, the rope groans—impossibly because there's nothing in his room to hang himself from but a flimsy light fixture. And in the vision it's a gruesome hemp rope, thicker than anything Father keeps coiled in our garage, rising through the ceiling into nothing. Or my brother's in bed, sheets sodden with blood, wrists and throat slit, face drained cold and blue. Or he's sitting in his reading chair with Father's rifle propped under his chin, about to poke the trigger with his naked toe; when I knock on his door and say, "Time for dinner, Paul."

As a family we never talked about what he had done or why. He never explained or apologized.

Mother claimed she took him for an evaluation, just after he'd jumped, and the psychiatrist or social worker or whoever diagnosed him merely with immaturity, and told her there was nothing to worry about. He'd grow out of it. It was an accident, and something we'd all be better off forgetting.

————

For years I heard him vomiting in the bathroom at night. Or upstairs in his room. The sound of his retching reverberating in the bones of the house. Usually he was just coughing.

As soon as I'd hear it though—*Oh no, oh no, oh no*, I'd speak in my mind in my bed, praying, *Please God, let Paul not be sick. Please God. Oh no, oh no, oh no* . . .

At twelve, thirteen, fourteen, I laid my head on a pillow that muffled my radio until the cartilage of my ear hurt. I kept the volume as low as could still be discerned—these whispers from the dictionary-size transistor with the telescopic antenna, retracted and clicked securely, with its black cord plugged into the dusty socket below my headboard.

At night I listened to 660 AM WFAN, "The Fan." Twenty-four-hour sports talk live from Secaucus, New Jersey, where Steve Somers, "graveyard DJ," would "rap" agreeably about any sport—horse racing, jai alai, darts—while leavening his commentary with reminiscences from a misspent youth in the '60s in the Haight and in Kashmir. The frequent caller "Bill from White Plains" was rumored to be a history teacher from my high school, who'd escaped Austria and the Holocaust via Shanghai as a child; he died raging with bitterness, I have heard, of lung cancer not long after these calls. "Good evening to you, and how you be? Steve Somers here and you there," he'd speak directly to me, to what felt like a handful of us, the insomniacs and the unemployed, the Holocaust survivors and cancer patients gathering around the campfire of his smoker's rasp. I drowned out the sound of my brother's phantasmal puking with the banter that would eventually lull me to sleep, and when I woke again, at any hour of the night, Steve Somers was still there, still talking.

"Play with him," Mother would press me if Paul had descended from his bedroom and was sitting on the floor of the den in front of the TV, tapping away at video games. While she disapproved of these games as masturbatory (though she'd never use that word), here was our chance: Paul was lonely—to a lethal degree—and she claimed I had the power to reach him.

She would observe us, folding laundry on the couch behind us, objecting when we said "I died" in the moment after our digital avatar had been defeated. It wasn't right, she'd say, how these games give away so many lives, and how these lost lives can then be so easily resumed with just the touch of a button. In real life one cannot "start over" when one is dead, she felt compelled to explain, as if Paul had tried to kill himself because of Nintendo. She urged us to say simply "I lost."

I too would feel a sinking shudder when Paul said "I died" or "I'm dead," and with that slow, slim smile, never involving his eyes, he'd touch the button and reset. I now noticed characters on TV and in movies talking glibly about suicide: "I could kill myself." "I want to die." And mental illness too: "Are you insane?" "Don't be nuts." "Let's go crazy!" Alone across the couch from him, a sob might swell in my throat before, mercifully, I succeeded in swallowing it down again.

Snowballs plunked in the fleeing folds of his misbuttoned coat. Or am I remembering another victim? Or was it him and was I one of his tormentors?

He played with me and my friends, boys five years younger, a generation in childhood terms. Fingering the trigger on a plastic Magnum, he popped the corner on the Peerys' driveway and heard Mitchell's drawl from high up, pot smoke drifting from Mitchell's bedroom window: "What are you *doing*, Paul? We start high school in the fall."

Most days Mitch Peery loitered beside the white-painted fence at the bottom of our dead-end street, until a conspicuous car drove down and around the turnaround. Idling, the driver would shake hands with Mitch through the open car window, eyes darting everywhere; then up the street the car would drive away. Mitch was a drug dealer, our father was sure, though his passion was bodybuilding. His muscles were bulbous. He might have been dealing steroids.

My brother was not athletic. He joined the track team, the sport of the socially maladjusted at our high school; cross-country was his event, and he ran in his grubby blue jeans. In the early miles of a long-distance practice he'd hang back and sneak into the Scarsdale Public Library, where the old men sat flipping through newspapers attached to wooden rods; and he'd read there too, one eye to the windows until his team came around again and he'd slip outside, seamlessly rejoining the tail end. He laughed when he told me about his ongoing deception.

His few friends were marginally less hopeless (one of them allegedly had a girlfriend). They played Dungeons & Dragons on the weekends. Our mother was conflicted: she approved of the salutary benefits of socializing, but D&D was demonstrably demonic (all those horned creatures!) and thereby, in concert with his violent video games, and his fantasy and science-fiction novels with their pre- and post-Christian moralities, at least partially responsible for his suicidality. So he kept his fun from her and spent his free time at his friends' homes, with his friends' families. He played hearts and gin rummy with Mr. and Mrs. Siegel at their kitchen table, for instance. It galled our mother terrifically that he liked his friends' families more than ours.

———

We must have felt insecure growing up in Scarsdale, with our father for a father, our mother would say. When we were old enough for summer jobs, our friends found themselves with internships in Manhattan arranged by their parents, and their parents' connections, but our father had no networks or nepotism at his disposal, Mother regretted to inform us. He was a disconnected man.

We remained in Scarsdale, she'd often tell us defensively, for the schools. "You *must* resent us though," she would bait us. "You *must* feel insecure." This was yet another of our mother's double binds; how could we resent who we came from, who we were? And to acknowledge our insecurity—not rich, not confident, not savvy—would be to admit that wealth and status mattered, or that we could never achieve these attributes on our own, in our own time. I wasn't then conscious of any sense of inferiority, only of a pressing need to prove myself—running for class president (and winning, at least in my first two years of high school), playing baseball and soccer through to the varsity level (a first among my siblings, though I played neither sport well), and then with my writing—my poems and stories and plays, seeking a refutation of my inadequacy from my readers or my audience.

While we couldn't blame Scarsdale for our problems, our mother could and often did. Our town, technically—and tweely—deemed a "village," was populated by sociopathic professionals, in her estimation, along with their enabling spouses and spoiled-rotten brats. Her concern was for us; there was too much pressure to succeed, socially and academically, to achieve a childhood trajectory toward adult fortune and fame. "Should we move?" she would ask me, in confidence, but I never answered honestly because I never believed it was an honest question.

One winter morning, as Mother was dropping me at school, a woman behind us honked her horn. We were taking too long. We were in the way. This was just the native rudeness that incensed her and Father: so entitled, condescending, combative! From the passenger seat I turned and flipped the driver the bird. The woman—somebody's mother—honked again with her mouth agape and her hands up like, What gives?

I stepped into the street: "Shut the fuck up!" Shocked, shaken, the woman drove slowly around us, without looking at us, and roared away. For years to come my mother would say she had never, before or since, felt so proud of a child of hers.

There is a violence in Scarsdale. *Scars* are the traces of trauma, of course, and that isolating *dale* serves to deepen, even pastoralize and normalize the connotation of pain in this place name. For a long time it seemed like everybody everywhere was quick to recall the 1980s Scarsdale Diet Doctor murder, when Jean Harris, a headmistress of a girls school in northern Virginia, shot and killed her two-timing paramour, Dr. Herman Tarnower, a cardiologist famous then for his *Complete Scarsdale Medical Diet*. (His house, the site of the murder, wasn't in Scarsdale, but his practice was.) In the 1970s there'd been that Yale student who cracked his girlfriend's skull with a hammer from her father's workbench—one of Father's old chestnuts. But it's suicide that stalks my hometown.

A mother of two, and a former school psychologist, parks her SUV in the right northbound lane of the Tappan Zee Bridge around noon on a Tuesday, steps into swerving and braking and howling horns, climbs onto the railing with her back to Manhattan, and drops 150 feet into the Hudson.

A middle-aged Scarsdalian jumps from the Henry Hudson Bridge in the Bronx to his death on the tracks below. A high school freshman throws himself in front of the commuter train as it rollicks into the Scarsdale station. A nineteen-year-old boy chains himself to a picnic table, then shoves the table and himself into the depths of the municipal diving pool. These are just some of the suicides that can be dredged up with a quick internet search.

I know of a boy from my graduating class who hanged himself not long after college, having moved home to live with his parents. A girl who used to inflame my adolescent libido with her leggings and her perm, bright pink gum snapping between her glossy lips—she grew up and got married and had two kids and moved to a town not far from Scarsdale, a town like Scarsdale; she got divorced, then killed herself recently. I don't know how or why.

Scarsdale has always seemed to me to cultivate desolations like these. But I was (and am) most likely projecting. My Scarsdale was almost entirely inside my house.

Paul's room was above mine, and I would hear his footsteps creaking along the floorboards, back and forth, back and forth overhead. I'd hear nothing for long stretches, when he was lying in bed, reading or crying or staring at his ceiling. He was languishing in his cell, as I was in mine below. After his suicide attempt I felt envious of this newfound, hard-won freedom of his to do nothing. He squirreled away junk food and soda; he bought himself a portable TV set the size of a World War II-era walkie-talkie.

Late at night he'd descend from his attic crypt like Nosferatu, creeping past my door and down the groaning stairs to the kitchen, leaving cupboard doors open and drawers wide so as to limit the noise, his spoon clinking in a bowl of dry cereal. In the afternoons he might vacate his room for one of his suspiciously long and steamy showers; or outside he'd go to mow the lawn, the only chore he was asked to carry out anymore. I'd hear the engine cord yanked, and yanked again until it caught, then smell the gas exhaust and fresh-cut grass. Making sure my movements went undetected by the others in the house, I'd slip upstairs to the attic and open the door.

His room was catastrophic: clothes piled on floor and fur-niture, no discernible distinction between clean and soiled (everything was tainted, judging by the odors). His vinyl shade was pulled down to the top of an air conditioner that dripped condensation like a ticking bomb. I would leave the overhead fluorescent light off as I picked my way through what felt like a crash site.

What was I searching for exactly? Evidence, I suppose. Drugs; Mother would ask me if I knew what drugs looked like and did I think Paul might be "hooked" on some? I found a disposable lighter in his dresser drawer, but no marijuana, not a single cigarette. I was hoping to uncover his next suicide note, or a draft of it. Or a journal like the one I kept, inun-dated with confessional poems like the poems I wrote. I never found anything more interesting than his porn, though.

Now I know that my brother's room smelled of semen: all those crusted socks and T-shirts. But for much of my life I couldn't quite place it, the stink, until one summer evening in rural Indiana at a writers' retreat, a gay colleague rhapsodized that the pollen drifting from the linden trees above "smelled like cum." "I don't think I know what that smells like," I confessed. That summer evening in Indiana had simply, if subliminally, put me in mind of my estranged brother's childhood bedroom.

He kept his magazines in a battered cardboard box at the

bottom of his closet and, bending over, I would—hands trembling—riffle through issues of *Playboy* and *Penthouse*; but also the rougher fare, the niche markets: lesbian, "shaved," barely legal, freakishly buxom, forty-plus, sixty-plus, sadomasochistic, sodomistic. Imagine my revulsion when I found myself handling a polyurethane sleeve meant to simulate for my brother the sensation of vaginal intercourse. (I was never tempted to use his device.)

And how did the porn get here in the first place? Surely not through the mail—our mother would have flagged any plain-brown-paper-wrapped magazines arriving in our mailbox. Had Paul brought them home from that engineering fraternity upstate where—wildly out of character—he'd apparently partied away his one semester of college, playing cards, drinking beer, never attending class? Maybe he'd pilfered them from the frat's lending library. Or he'd bought them himself at newsstands outside Grand Central or in Times Square, where I'd seen the covers of such shocking magazines myself, the few times I'd been allowed to visit the city with friends. I didn't understand how he could bear the embarrassment, buying these magazines from strangers.

Joyce worked part-time at the Georgetown University bookstore. When she learned of Paul's collection, she told me that the students who bought dirty magazines from her were losers, pathetic and to be pitied.

But by then I was already borrowing from my brother's library, taking one issue at a time down to my room. I'd keep it overnight like a rendezvous, before sneaking it (her?) back into my brother's closet the next day. At first I chose from the bottom of his box, the magazines he'd be less likely to notice missing, but quickly I realized it didn't matter. He didn't notice, or if he did notice he didn't care. He never said a word to me. We never talked anymore anyway. So I grew bolder, then reckless, borrowing several magazines at a time and sliding them between my mattress and my box spring like a personal, two-dimensional harem.

And through it all I was torturing myself, confessing my sin in prayer and begging God for forgiveness. I would promise never to pollute my soul with those images again, or to abuse the temple of my body with something as craven and ghoulish as masturbation. I was at that time a literalist when it came to God's smiting of Onan for "spilling his seed," so I feared retribution. And I agonized that my sperm, lingering microscopically in the bathtub, could somehow impregnate my prepubescent sister. I would manage to abstain for weeks, then months at a time, and I'd begin to feel pure, superior . . . until succumbing again. I sensed already that self-abasement in itself was the temptation.

Soon I was bringing my brother's magazines to school and leaving them there, one at a time. Was I saving myself? Saving him? I smuggled my secret from the house as if it were a changeling, or the heart of a vampire, an object so vile and damnable stowed in my backpack with my binders and textbooks, and at every turn I thrilled at the possibility of discovery. Unzipping and removing my sin—our sin—I'd hold it for a moment breathless in the open air before chucking it inside a school dumpster, or discarding it in the woods nearby. I was returning a debt, closing a circle. One time in the library I slid a copy of *Hustler* between volumes of poetry and walked away, feeling they belonged together. I meant this as a joke.

We were watching TV. Paul had his legs crossed, bouncing his foot nervously on his knee. Mother reminded him that it was his night to do the dishes and he replied like Bartleby that he simply preferred not to. *Why does it have to be me?* he seemed to be asking. *Or any of your kids? Why can't you do anything for yourself?* An instantly vicious argument spilled upstairs to their bedroom, where Father had been reading in bed.

"Fuck you!"

"That's it," Father was shouting too. "Let it all out!"

"Fuck you!" Paul spat his words.

"That's how you've always felt about us—your own parents! You hate us! Admit it!"

I stood at the foot of the stairs, flexing the new sinews in my adolescent arms. I felt strong enough now to defend my family, to kill my brother, if it came to that.

But why couldn't he pretend? Why wouldn't he hold his tongue and withstand my parents, this family, with patience, with cunning? Then he might survive. That was my plan, at least.

On my sixteenth birthday he left home for an attic apartment in Yonkers. He was twenty. We kept a lot of his things, including his pornography, in boxes in the basement where it often flooded after rain, linoleum buckling loose, exposing the corrugated cement beneath. Those Tupperware buckets of rice, honey, wheat, yeast, and powdered milk—our apocalypse supplies, untouched—still lined the room's steel shelves.

Father had stacked Paul's boxes on the floor, sealed with duct tape and labeled with black marker. I found it odd, and still do, that he would choose to save his son's pornographic magazines, as if Paul might return home at any moment to reclaim them. As if they were important mementos like his yearbooks and his kindergarten art. I didn't know why Paul hadn't taken his magazines with him in the first place, or thrown them out. At the time I wondered if he'd left them behind for me.

———

As we marched across a burning stretch of beach on the Cape, laden with folding chairs and umbrellas and a cooler or two, Father mentioned offhand to me that Paul would never marry. He didn't elaborate and I didn't respond.

"Is your brother gay?" Mother asked as we drove in her car together and alone. Paul wasn't effeminate. And his magazines were straight.

"I don't think so," I answered as she stared blankly through the windshield.

I suppose Mother wondered whether Paul meant to persuade himself with his pornography; was his depression deepened by a conflicted or complicated desire?

I wondered this too. But probably as usual when worrying about my brother I was worrying about myself.

Once, when I assumed I would never see my brother again, I was driving north from Manhattan and found myself pulling off the parkway. I wanted to visit our house, now a home for strangers. I considered introducing myself as one of those revenants I remember from childhood who'd materialize at our front door, asking, "Can I come in? I grew up here . . . My God, everything looks so small!"

But I lacked the courage, or the will. Driving slowly in my rental car down the dead end to the turnaround—conspicuous, no doubt a shady character. Mrs. Taggart, wrinkled and wreathed now with cottony hair, squinted at me over the loop of her splashing garden hose. Our house looked the same. Smaller, yes. Neater. But haunted still. I couldn't stop.

I drove to the Village Hall next, where Paul had been working as Scarsdale's high-tech guru since he dropped out of college in the early '90s, and I parked beside his car, a black Pontiac Fiero (so he still drove it!) cluttered inside with trash from takeout, as it had always been, a remote-controlled hot rod and assorted other gadgets on the passenger seat. I was on my way to rehearsals at a theatre festival in New England. And in that moment—staring at the toys in his car, anticipating several weeks of toying around with yet another of my nonprofit "plays"—I pitied us both: brothers who hadn't grown up, could not grow up. I wondered for the first time why I was writing at all, before the threat of actually seeing my brother again sent me on my way.

We sat down for a meal together, something we'd never done before, as adults or as kids, several years ago now at the Metro Diner in Scarsdale, around the corner from the train station, where Paul told me he would never have children due to the expense. He didn't mention—he's never mentioned—a lover or partner of any kind, and I've never asked.

It was lunchtime but he would "do the scrambled eggs and bacon—crispy," he instructed the waitress, with a slight pinching gesture of his fingers. When I ordered a garden burger and an Amstel Light, he chuckled nervously, perhaps teasingly.

I was surprised, though I shouldn't have been, to see that he'd grown stout and bald like our father; his face was pale and blemished like a teenager. I'd emailed that I was researching this book. I couldn't remember the last time we'd seen each other. Ten years had passed, at least. Interviewing him was the only way I could face him, and I forced myself that day to speak honestly. To begin, I confessed that I'd long assumed he hated me, because I had been the golden child, or I'd believed I was, and he was the opposite of me. He chuckled nervously again.

We compared medications. I considered myself stable enough on a fairly low dose of Zoloft, and Paul ticked off a trio I didn't recognize. He attributed his weight gain and dry mouth to the drugs. "The point is, we all need to figure out which drugs work best for us," I said, and he laughed—agreeably this time.

He clarified some things, muddled others. He buried those dead raccoons by himself, he corrected me. And Uncle Brian said goodbye to him on the morning of his disappearance, he was sure of it: he was the only one awake, playing Chinese checkers with himself. One night, years later, Brian called him, he said, or called our house but only Paul was home, and our uncle was drunk and incoherent. He apologized without saying what it was he was sorry for. When I shared my theory—my fantasy, I admitted, hedging—that Brian might be my true father, Paul exploded with enthusiasm: "That would be *awesome!*"

Before lunch Paul had given me a quick tour of his new apartment on Garth Road, the address for the "newly wed and nearly dead," as Father often said, though surely confirmed bachelors of any age have long been denizens of this mildly urban neighborhood. Paul had only last month signed the deed. A cinematic flat-screen was mounted on his wall, a state-of-the-art game console was strewn across the floor; clear tarping protected pieces of blocky modern furniture. One side of the apartment overlooked the train tracks that carried commuters to and from Grand Central; other windows opened on the workaday street where trees kindled with autumn light and leaves. An Amtrak express came thundering past, and Paul raised his voice, "My friend Jocelino is painting the place for me!" I was surprised to learn he had a friend. Ben Siegel, from high school, had bailed Paul out of the hospital after one of his relapses, but Ben lived and worked in the city, where Paul wouldn't go anymore—"All those people . . ." he said to me in his shadowy kitchen, shaking his head disapprovingly, sounding a lot like our father.

Jocelino called, as if on cue, and Paul answered: "No, everything looks great, Jocelino—just great!" The new colors (beige and gray) on the old walls looked "really, really great!" Something about the way he reassured Jocelino, with ease and affection, and how he mentioned my name as if he'd done so before—"I'm showing my brother Danny the apartment"— made me wonder if I'd been wrong about him all these years. Maybe he hadn't been lonely at all. Maybe he'd simply succeeded in living a life free of us, his family.

Our father came for him once in the parking lot of the Village Hall. Paul hadn't spoken to him in years—to either of our parents, in fact. (I was still speaking to them then, but barely.) They'd moved to Virginia the year before. Paul had gone to visit Joyce in Maryland that Thanksgiving, and afterward she told our parents that he was looking worse than ever, overweight and unhealthy. She was concerned. Father knew his son wouldn't return his calls, or had been ignoring his calls already; he ambushed Paul as he came prancing down the wide concrete steps from the Village Hall, as he'd pranced down the stairs as a boy in our house. A streetlight in the parking lot blinked on.

"Paul?"

And what did he say in response? "Hi," or anything? How could he? Father would tell Mother, and Mother would tell me, that Paul simply turned his back on our father, walked to his black Fiero, and drove away.

"Your father says he doesn't look half bad," Mother told me. "It's true he's heavier. He's lost his hair. But that's normal for a man his age."

But why did he walk away? I asked. Did she know? "He's angry. He's always been angry at us."

Mother had long ago dismissed Paul's mental illness as an excess of anger. She often invoked a self-help definition of suicide as "anger turned inward." If only Paul had exorcised his anger at his parents, as unjustified as it was, maybe he wouldn't have wanted to end his life.

When I was newly diagnosed with cancer a Russian acupuncturist in Venice Beach told me that my anger had caused it. Something to do with a misalignment of my Manipura chakra, the point above the navel, roughly where the sutures were holding my belly together at the time. Anger unspoken causes cancer in organs: "specifically the bowel." Her metaphor offended me. We'd just met. I was weak from the surgery, and I lost my temper. I told her she was peddling medieval horseshit, and hobbled out of her office without a single needle of hers pricking my skin. I had spent my entire adult life giving voice to my emotions—anger often foremost, but also longing, regret, loneliness, love; in my quiet way I had been expressing everything in the belief that it was this expression that would save my life.

But sometimes I think she's right. As a man I should have shouted like my father—should be shouting now about my cancer and my wife's cancer, about the unfairness of it all, with rage and defiance. As a boy I should have been crying out constantly for the love I was being denied. Or, like my brother Paul, I should have leapt from our attic window myself, for although his act horrified me then, I knew it was in its way a tour de force of honesty. I was afraid of what he'd done because I admired it.

His report card that afternoon was full of Cs and Ds. Another mother would have wondered why her smartest child, with the highest IQ and near-perfect SATs, had apparently stopped studying. Why he stayed in his room, washed himself infrequently.

She railed at him in the kitchen, waving the slip of paper in his face. She would tell Father when he came home. She took me to the grocery store. Sally, almost six, and baby Tommy must have come with us. Steven too? Conspicuously I remember only Mother and me leaving in the car together.

No matter how it happened, Paul was left alone. I'd learn afterward that he walked all over the house, contemplating other methods: razor blades from Father's basement workbench, that heavy rope in the garage, a rifle.

He chose to jump. "From the roof," as Steven told me later, though it turned out he'd jumped from a window just beneath it. Still, as a symbol, as poetry, it worked: Paul climbed to the pinnacle of our excruciating home, a scapegoat for the family's sin of failing him.

What courage did it take, what pity, to unscrew the quarter-moon window from its frame? (A window that looked like one of two eyes in the face of the house.) And had it been screwed shut, actually? And what for? Or did Father only secure it after the fact, to deter a repeat performance? There were no hinges, one couldn't open the window without removing the frame and leaning it against the wall, as Paul did, on the carpet, beneath this sudden hole sighing violently with wind. So yes, there had been a screwdriver resting on the desk, as I saw later. Was the neighborhood quiet? Did a neighbor come or go below? Crows cawed. Where was Father this whole time? Amazingly, unfortunately, he had work someplace that day.

Paul was small but the window was smaller and he had to poke his leg through, straddling the short sill; then ducking his head and heaving his chest out; then the other leg, bracing hands inside the frame. Then the cold air, wisps of ragged breath, the sun caught in bare branches, Paul readying himself to topple like a tear from the house's open eye. With tears in his eyes. Or not—dry and dedicated: here was his purpose, his answer.

Or was it quick and meaningless, first his leg, through and out, then his head, losing balance and . . . he slipped into the mistake of a lifetime?

The nothing is easily crossed. Three stories should have been enough; he would have been fortunate to break a leg, or his spine. What broke his fall, then? The snow on this shaded side of the house was a scab of February thaw. He fell through brittle fanning evergreen until slamming home. Scratched and bruised and his breath knocked out.

Clouds were crossing the sky. Crows mocked him.

That night Mother cried in my arms at the top of the attic stairs. She made me make that promise to never tell a soul, to die with this secret if I loved her. I promised. Then she was happy: "An angel caught him as he fell," she swore, "and laid him out gently in the snow."

"He's alive," she said, shaking her head; she could not believe it. And he is still living today.

Enormous Wings

She saw my pain before I did; before I knew what it was, my mother knew that my pain had a plan, or a name at least, and she shared what she knew with me.

I was categorizing my fears as they proliferated unchecked, following a secret order in how I sought order. I cycled through everything: stepped carefully across a minefield of lines between tiles and sidewalk cracks; washed my hands until cracks opened in them, until they bled; counted footsteps and flipped switches; synced my glances at the corners of my bedroom ceiling to the rhythm of a song—any song, it didn't matter—bouncing around the corners of my brain. I touched things and people sparingly, and with regret. A stealthy perfectionist, I hid it well, or thought I did, swearing and wrestling with friends on the school bus while inwardly I worked my way through my intricate prayers, asking God for forgiveness. I was scrupulous. I slept with my hands laced in prayer, as atonement for these perpetually recurring, personal sins, but also to forestall the nuclear apocalypse that was at every moment imminent. When I woke in the morning my fingers throbbed as they tightly and ever-so-slightly uncurled.

In the dark of a dinner theatre in Elmsford, where she'd taken her three oldest boys for a treat, while the Clancy Brothers pattered and sang their shtick in those stupid Aran sweaters, my mother gently pulled my hands apart. She had noticed I was praying. She saw my shame, and she knew that my shame only fueled more prayer.

Soon I craved the pleasure of confessing to her, the coiled spring of repression released in a moment of forgiveness, of reprieve. "How can I be sure I'm *not* dying?" I'd ask her. "How can I know for certain that I'm *not* possessed by demons—even by Satan?"

I surrendered to her the Swiss Army knife that Father had given me for my twelfth birthday, because I saw the blood of my family spattered and smeared across the walls of our house. It was a premonition, I told her tearfully. My sleepwalking self would do it.

She must have panicked—one son suicidal, and another losing his mind. Was I disintegrating into schizophrenia like her brother had, so many years ago?

"You want control," she explained, hoping to convince me, and herself. "What Paul has done has made you feel chaotic—like anything can happen—and your brain is struggling to compensate, to impose order on chaos."

She prescribed a self-therapy of self-expression. The act of writing would cure me.

"Take this," she said, handing me a book with blank pages and a pen, "and write it all down. Anything frightening, uncontrollable. Write it down and pick it up and carry it with you into the world." I loved her for this gift.

I climbed the stairs to the attic and what had been Joyce's bedroom (she was away at college by now, and Paul hadn't yet moved up here) to sit at my mother's manual typewriter, with the letters at the ends of spindly bars that would jam in a metal fist when I poked too rapidly. I can still feel in my fingertips the delicately ticking knob as I rolled the paper in (I used her ivory linen résumé sheets when I could, hoping she wouldn't notice; and she didn't, or didn't care, or she tacitly approved), then snapping the metal bracer down, the inky ribbon smudging, that Pavlovian *ding* inducing my headlong, racketing returns. Soon enough I was switching on her electric model, and feeling the hum in my hands, and watching my rapid-fire text unspool. Then later still I wrote alone in Father's office across the hallway at night (Paul had flunked out of college and was living in Joyce's room now) on the suitcase-sized "portable" Osborne computer, with the black passport-sized screen and goblin-green type, my outpouring transmitting through a gray cable into the waist-high dot-matrix machine. Then, while the family below watched TV, I'd tear along the perforations, pare the sprocket holes away, until I held in my hands my poem, my story, my self.

Mother mailed my work to the *New Yorker*, and the pre-printed slips seemed to bounce back to us instantaneously. She couldn't understand how these editors could be so ignorant, she said. I wonder now what she could have been thinking; surely she didn't believe that what I was writing at twelve or thirteen was worthy of publication in any adult magazine, much less in the *New Yorker*. She was this naïve. Or it wasn't encouragement she was offering but slyly its opposite.

With high school and puberty I was writing more dedicatedly and darkly. I dared not share these poems and stories with my mother. Words were coming unbidden like visitations or possessions, like one passage I remember vividly, scribbled as if automatically, about discovering my identical twin, beaten and discarded bloodied in a red azalea bush. Here was my subconscious, or something stranger, warning me—but of what? (I was capable of frightening myself with what I wrote, and I still can, when I'm lucky.) When I was done for the evening, I would descend from the attic to my bedroom to bury what I'd written in a pallet piled with books and magazines at the foot of my bed: hidden from my mother, or so I thought.

I read compulsively, but not like Paul who devoured sci-fi and fantasy only, his Del Rey paperbacks splayed facedown on the carpet of his room to save his place until the bindings turned a squeaking, striated white. Steven hardly read at all, but his math and science grades were good. I scavenged what Joyce brought home from college, risking carsickness one summer to read her dog-eared, underlined, marginalia-crammed copy of *Waiting for Godot* on our way north toward the tribulation of yet another family vacation—this time at Dr. Linden's loose-pill-riddled cottage overlooking Lake Caspian in the redneck northeast kingdom of Vermont. Saddened by *Godot*, I recognized it subverbally: here was the theatre of my childhood, an absurd, never-ending performance both disguising and laying bare a story devoid of meaning—that is, a family devoid of affection. What I have read in the years since of Samuel Beckett's family, and of his mother in particular, has not altered my early opinion of his masterwork, or of his oeuvre, for that matter.

And then there was W. B. Yeats (pronounced to rhyme with "Keats") and these lines from "Remorse for Intemperate Speech" that have remained for me indelible:

> Great hatred, little room
> Maimed us at the start.
> I carry from my mother's womb
> A fanatic heart.

In this, my fanatic youth, I was lonely in the crowded country of my family, and maimed by hatred too, or at least by anger—my parents' anger, my siblings', my own. "Out of Ireland have we come" is the line preceding, so I knew I would be returning to Ireland one day (despite never having been there before).

From the library my mother brought home *Writers on Writing: A Bread Loaf Anthology*, edited by the pleasingly alliterative pair of professors Pack and Parini; I aspired to be their student one day at Middlebury College in Vermont (and I was).

Mother's anthology of the modern short story, a remainder from her continued-ed career, introduced me to Joyce Carol Oates riffing on Bob Dylan in "Where Are You Going, Where Have You Been?" I knew where I was and where, at least, I wanted to go, and I knew that writing was how I would get there, or anywhere. One story in that anthology inspired years of imitation: Gabriel García Márquez's "A Very Old Man with Enormous Wings"; I read García Márquez—or tried to read him, and others, like Carlos Fuentes, Mario Vargas Llosa, Miguel de Unamuno—in Spanish. The vague and vaguely racist term "magical realism" seemed to apply to my childhood, living as I did in a family that believed in many things that were not real, while disbelieving what was real.

I wrote my first real poem about Paul. Entitled "Snow," it was influenced—to the precipice of plagiarism—by Langston Hughes's "My Friend" and Ezra Pound's "In a Station of the Metro":

My brother tried to kill himself.
There's nothing more to say.

Just like raindrops
On a shaking black bough,
He pushed us all—
Thank God for snow.

Despite my efforts to keep my adolescent writing under wraps, my mother read my journal when I wasn't home, and when we fought she'd use this kompromat against me. If I questioned how she'd attained this information about my love life, or my feelings about her, she would credit a maternal clairvoyance whereby she could not help but pluck my secrets out of the turbid ether of our home because—how else?—"a mother knows."

She didn't inhibit me; she influenced me. I wrote more but smaller, literally, my handwriting shrinking, as if miniaturizing my words might safeguard them. When I learned from teachers that the books esteemed greatest were often the most difficult to understand—modern if not postmodern (which certainly sounded like an improvement to me)—I resolved never to write plainly, sinking my confessions instead inside miasmas of overelaboration, and an idiosyncratic code called style, my stories and poems left to be deciphered by my future (!) readers.

Parentheses proliferated (I required parentheses within parentheses (within parentheses (to be certain I was telling the truth, or digging doggedly toward it))). I deploy(ed) semicolons erroneously; colons recklessly: every sentence happened to be also on-the-other-hand. Seeing things from both sides, from all sides, was how I aimed to climb the crooked narrow path uphill toward the summit of literary achievement. I ended up constructing labyrinths instead, like Jorge Luis Borges, another of my early heroes. But my labyrinths were amateurish and insolvable.

My mother professed an inability to appreciate the writers I admired: James Joyce, Samuel Beckett, William Faulkner, T. S.

Eliot. Perhaps she pretended because perplexity was easier (and sneakier) than outright disapproval. But was she mocking me? "What is 'stream-of-consciousness,' Danny? What on earth is 'magical realism?'" And she would conclude our harried salons á deux with this, her characteristic rebuke: "But tell me—why does good writing have to be *so sad*?"

I did not get along with my high school teachers. Poor Ms. Hummel, who, still in her twenties and dating the dashing Mr. Katz, took me to task one day for writing in the voice of Ponce de León; she called my essay "racially insensitive" (it was) and made me read it aloud to the class (where, in my defense, it killed as comedy). In revenge I wrote Ms. Hummel an erotic poem about sunflower seeds with a blatant subtext of cunnilingus. (The poem was printed in our high school lit mag *Jabberwocky*—with a great deal of excitement on the part of the editors—spread across the stapled centerfold pages.) Fey, brown-suited Mr. Flanagan in Honors English found my analytical voice "flip" and my creative excursions infuriatingly inchoate; on the last page of my stories he would simply scrawl a long languid question mark, along with that most devastating of pedantic criticisms: "See me." And I would see him, ready for a fight, in his office after school, where we'd argue exhaustingly about whether or not I had the right, in his opinion, to write that a window in a drizzle was "sweating." And so forth. I don't know what meaning or pleasure he was deriving from these arguments. He called me, and all boys, his "dear boy." *Jude the Obscure*, he bragged, was the only book for him, and he reread it every year. A colleague of his, many years later, told me: "We all knew he had a crush on you."

Whenever I published in *Jabberwocky* I would leave the magazine lying around the house, on the dining room table or kitchen counter. Mother might pick it up and read my poem or story, but she'd never say she liked it; she wouldn't say anything at all, unless asked, and then through pursed lips: "Why can't you write about *happy* things, Danny?"

"Life isn't happy," I would reply with the arrogance of youth.

"You're going to be a writer," she'd respond, though her oft-repeated prophecy was beginning to sound a lot like condemnation. "Whatever you do, though, don't write about me. Don't write about us, Danny, your family." Then after a moment's reflection: "I know you will anyway."

I suspected that she wanted me to write about her "anyway." I didn't understand, but I felt her projecting or injecting an almost libidinal desire for exposure, for confession, for perception and sympathy into me. I would do for her what she would not or could not do for herself. She was ambivalent, of course; for beneath her pretended bafflement, her Pollyannaish critique of what I'd written, my mother was developing a savage envy that we would both labor long to ignore.

In high school my anxiety flowered and I fell out of favor with friends. I was touchy and self-serious. I was an artist. They were jocks. When I acted in my first play in high school they asked, "So what are you now, a faggot?"

I stayed home on weekends when they didn't call, reading *Portrait of the Artist as a Young Man* and *The Sound and the Fury*. If they invited me along to a party, or to share a case of cheap beer in Butler Woods, more often than not I would say: "I can't. I've got work to do."

"What work?"

"Writing."

"Writing what?" they would ask, and "What for?"

But not writing only; performance would save me too. I wanted to entertain.

It began with humiliation. Telling some joke over and over, as children do, until Father above me snapped, "Shut up, Danny. It's not funny anymore."

But it was. Simply because he'd found it unfunny, agitating even—this would become the point of my jokes with him, then with the world.

Not long after Paul tried to kill himself we all started to eat dinner together because Mother had gleaned from her self-help books that children need a stable family unit. So our dining room table became nightly a stultifying lie of normality. Mother despised how Father chewed, too much and too loudly, how he hunched and picked at the iceberg lettuce with his fork. Paul's lubricious mouth sounds turned her stomach too. Father for his part ignored Mother down there at the end of the table, unless it was to ask without looking, "Where'd you get this meat?"—though Mother often said she'd only given us food poisoning once, when we were young so what was the big deal anyway?—or to ridicule her for saying something "idiotic." He'd shake his head with infinite condescension if she forgot, yet again, to serve with the chicken his cranberry sauce, sloughed out of the tin can and sliced with a butter knife (only Father liked the stuff; Steven ate it but he ate anything). Joyce, if she was visiting from college, would just sit there, irrelevantly nervous. Paul would say nothing while staring at nothing, and nothing was across the table where I sat, so he stared at me or through me at the beige wallpaper with the hateful non-expression of the incarcerated, answering any question lobbed his way with one word—one syllable, if he could manage it. A thatch of dark chest hairs sprouted in the gaping collar of his Izod; the seat of his pants or summer shorts stuck lightly to the seat of the wooden chair when he fidgeted or stood, and we would snicker behind his back: Such execrable hygiene! which shouldn't have been funny because if he wasn't washing—his body or his clothes—then chances were high he was considering suicide again. Sally chirping beside Mother, baby Tommy on Mother's other side refusing wisely to eat, while I did everything I could to undermine our father with my jokes at his expense, especially when he had just barked something cruel about minorities or women or gays, or about his own wife and children. The closer I cut to his bone the better—and the funnier. I made the long table laugh, or titter at least, the whole captive audience of our large unhappy family. Even my father would chuckle, as if he hadn't understood himself to be the butt of my joke, or he did understand but he didn't have the wit to retaliate. I played the fool to his thickheaded Lear at the dining room table, just as I would in my life moving forward, because he was right: it wasn't funny anymore.

She was driving me to school. I'd let her read my latest story—about a girl who suffers a breakdown after a clandestine abortion (what did I know of these things?)—and my mother didn't like it. Five years had passed since Paul had done what he'd done.

"Why do you return to these things? Why do you hold on to them? Why do you *dwell*?" It was a plea to do what she could not do herself. "Why can't you simply forget?"

I was seventeen. I was a loner though I had a girlfriend, somebody as melancholic as me. I was biding my time, reading and writing during free periods beneath a cement gargoyle outside the emergency exit near the English classrooms.

My mother drove more hazardously than usual that morning—tapping through stop signs, barreling around corners. She wasn't watching where she was going, her mind and mouth running elsewhere.

She stopped the car across the Post Road from school. Through the window the breeze tousled a sunny profusion of leaves and flowers. She would not turn to look at me. Whatever I was about to say to justify myself and my writing would never be enough. But I was young and still believed that what I wrote could win her love. As I got out of the car she allowed me to kiss her cheek; she was a statue of a saint, she was the Madonna. I can still feel her coldness on my lips.

First Love

I CONJURED HER beside me in the back seat of the family wagon as we drove home one summer from the Cape: whoever she was or would be. Just as in the months before her birth I would conjure the body and breath of the daughter who would soon wear the tiny clothes I hung neatly in what was now her closet. Two times I have fallen in love with ghosts of my future.

She was tragically inclined, like me, and attractive, or "striking," as a closeted gay teacher remarked, after he'd seen us canoodling against the lockers outside his office. He seemed impressed but skeptical.

She cut her hair short, close to a crew cut, save for a thin braid that dangled like a rat's tail upon her downy nape. She was petite, like my mother; she was a feminist, unlike my mother. She ran track, hurdled, the steeplechase. She swam as well. She was far too beautiful, in my opinion, and that of many others, to be so solitary and shy. She was perfect for me, a near-twin to fix or to suffer with.

She was Roman Catholic and she wore a silver cross around her neck. Her father's and mother's parents were immigrants from Cyprus and Poland respectively. Her father had been a priest and her mother a nun when they fell in love (he was a history teacher in Port Chester now, and she was a sigh-heavy teacher's aide at the high school in Mamaroneck). She had three sisters, two older and one younger, all pretty and artistic and touchy. I noticed her sitting alone one morning atop the high wall at Maria Regina High School in Hartsdale, where we attended driver's ed, as I rolled by in the back seat of Neil Matthews' Taurus, Guns N' Roses blaring. I knew at that moment I would be leaving my friends for her.

Because she did, I worked part-time at Baxter's Farm, a fruit-and-veg stand beside a suburban driveway with a front-yard pumpkin patch in fall, and greenhouses and gardens out back. Old Farmer Baxter, suffering from skin cancer, sat across the driveway at his dining room window, veiled behind lace curtains, keeping an eye on his junior greengrocers. His wife Freja, rumored to have been a mail-order bride in the '50s, was our forewoman, but she'd spend hours each day cutting flowers out back, hoping to lower her blood pressure. (Not so many years later she'd sneeze in a local Chinese restaurant and die on the spot of a stroke.) I bagged and worked the register, arguing with housewives about whether I'd knowingly sold them bruised tomatoes yesterday (likely I had), and juggling potatoes during rain showers to provoke laughter in the girl I desired.

Those winter weeks in the new year leading up to our first kiss in her father's spotless Tercel, parked along snow-silenced streets, playing the mix tape she'd made for me with "Suite: Judy Blue Eyes" (though she had brown eyes): I'd kissed a few girls, but never like this. We used the word *love* right away. Weeknights in the attic at my father's desk I would pick up the phone on the first ring, then while absently rearranging his mechanical pencils and metal engineering rulers, swiveling minutely in his "executive's chair," I'd talk to her for hours, gazing up through the skylights at the moon and stars, or the clouds and rain, or the snow slowly occluding the glass.

I could not wait to tell her my secrets: my brother's suicide attempt, my parents' ancient sorrows and current cruelties. She said she'd been teased and bullied for that cross around her neck, and groped by older boys in a junior high bathroom once. She suspected an elderly German babysitter had abused her as a toddler—physically or sexually, she wasn't sure— because her parents came home one evening to find her trembling behind the sofa. She dreamed of her grandfather's death but failed to warn the family and he died of a heart attack days later, and her guilt drove her to contemplate swallowing a bottle of aspirin. She fell apart confessing this last secret, as I held her in the front seat of my mother's station wagon, parked beneath a streetlight beside an empty playground. I had known already she was in some ways ineffably like my mother, but now, with a sinking heart, I recognized her as my brother too.

Sundays we drove past my mother's mansion to Larchmont to sit in the sun on the black rocks above the Sound, where in our matching black books I would write my poems and she would sketch. She was going to be a fashion designer. Already she made her own clothes, like the splashy blue-sequined flapper number she wore as my date to the prom. She ate "low-fat" and "all-natural" foods. Her politics were, like mine, progressive; we staunchly opposed the Persian Gulf War. Her grades were good but not great. Her anxiety ruined her for tests. I asked her to be my girlfriend on Valentine's Day, the day after the anniversary of my brother's leap from the attic window, and she said yes.

On one of our first dates a cop pulled us over—I didn't know why. I was a new driver. My hands were shaking as I lifted them from the wheel. But I knew I had been caught and

I was guilty. How did I ever think I could get away with this? I thought, whatever this was . . . It was a dead taillight.

My mother asked me one night as I was leaving to pick up my girlfriend: "Is it true some men have bigger penises?"

"Bigger?" I asked.

"Bigger than other men's."

She told me that Tommy, seven years old and sitting beside her at the kitchen table, had just told her so. He was smiling, quietly aghast. Was she joking? I wondered. Was this a trick? I answered honestly: "More or less."

This was the entirety of my mother's sex talk with me. Three years earlier, in the overcast mugginess of the outdoor courtyard at Steven's high school graduation, I was fourteen and inexplicably erect. The erection was more exciting than the ceremony. My mother must have felt sleepy when she dropped her program into the grass at my feet; before I could adjust myself she was reaching down between my knees, and her forearm brushed my hardness. She glanced sidelong at me. I'd never seen her at a loss for words. Then up straight she sat, as if paying rapt attention to the valedictorian speaker, as he articulated his vision of our limitless future.

We secluded ourselves in the den, watching movies we'd rented for the evening (not planning to watch them), and after my family had fallen asleep, or at least gone upstairs to bed, we'd fool around. We planned to lose our virginities to each other, but the few times we tried she would cry and say her stomach hurt. She was too Catholic, we both agreed. Late one evening, leaving to drive her home, we were shocked to find my father sitting silently in the dark in the living room like a sentry. He said nothing as we mumbled good night.

Years later I learned from my brother Paul that my parents were convinced I would get my high school girlfriend pregnant. It had happened to them so why not to me? (Not that they would admit that their oldest child Joyce—and the whole toppling cascade of our births, in a sense—had been an accident.) But they needn't have worried. When my girlfriend and I attempted to have sex we used a condom; we were teenagers of the AIDS pandemic, after all. (For his part the only counsel my father ever gave me concerning sex was: "I don't want this girl's father calling me in the middle of the night.")

I was so happy with her that I would often cry. Not from happiness but dread; the happier I felt, the closer I heard my doom approaching, like thunderheads rumbling just over the horizon.

Her parents seemed to like me well enough, but my parents ignored her. My mother interpreted her shyness as snobbery and she judged her whole family as unambitious. After spotting my girlfriend's mother at the grocery, my mother came home and complained, "That mousy woman just scurried away from me."

My first semester of college my girlfriend came to visit. We clung to each other on the vinyl mattress napping, sweetly holding each other's genitals; we had sex. Afterward she cried, and I blamed myself. I deserved this.

From the beginning I had hid my misgivings. She was slightly more antisocial than me; she was jealous of my friends, what friends I had. She envied my bucolic, expensive liberal arts college (she underrated herself and enrolled in a suitcase school in New Jersey). She both admired and resented my conviction that I'd spend my life writing. I grew to find her misery depressingly familiar, and I felt burdened by it, incapable of curing it.

I broke up with her many times, over many years, and each time she'd fall to pieces, unhinged even. She'd spend long nights in the emergency room vomiting from heartache and panic. Then back home in Scarsdale in the summer during college, she and I would find ourselves alone together again. We were all and everything the other one had. And when I left for Ireland after college, she followed me.

We were alone there together too, again, but exotically so. In dank pubs I spoke honestly and cruelly of the girl I had fallen in love with (who was still in college, still dating somebody else anyway, but never mind). By Christmas she dropped out of her art school in county Kildare and flew home to Scarsdale. I never saw her again. I'm relieved, for her sake and mine, that we didn't marry.

What I find myself remembering often is leaving her, or dropping her off rather, on the far side of town; then driving alone through the stilled suburban neighborhoods. If a light burned somewhere then a drama like my family's was playing out inside. Spring turning into summer, with the breeze off the golf course ruffling the hairs on my arm in the open window, my free hand palming the side mirror . . . I was on my way home for the night but not for long.

The Ache

MY STOMACH HURT at a restaurant in the Berkshires—that summer's getaway: more time with Father, time for him to complain about the food, humiliate our waitresses for inattentiveness or overattentiveness.

I was ruining everything that early evening. She removed me from the table. She was put out. Was I "whining" again? In the parked car she sat up front and rolled her window down; I curled into the footwell and lifted my shirt to soothe my belly against the warm upholstery. "It's gas," my mother was dismissive. We were missing dinner. The myriad arms of the flourishing trees seemed to sway above me in celebration.

The ache was like a hand grasping me inside and squeezing. No, like two hands seizing and twisting my intestines like a rag. Then respite; shame in the reflecting bowl. A wisp of mucus, a blot of blood; before the cramping kicked in again.

I was sick. A stomach bug without nausea or vomiting. No fever. But nobody else in the house felt unwell. She told me to go to bed and stay there—or I told myself, knowing that I should. This was the summer before college, and she'd been angrier with me than ever; for writing love poems, for falling in love. She ordered me to break up with my girlfriend, which only ensured that we would stay together longer than we would or should have otherwise.

That last summer, with neighbors' doors slamming and lawn mowers and leaf blowers droning, the helplessness of infancy revived in the languor of my sickroom. *Bringing It All Back Home* played tinnily in the diminutive boom box on my night table. My girlfriend dawdled in the foyer at the foot of the stairs, and I would descend for a sympathetic assignation on the living room couch, while Mother banged and gonged her simmering disapproval from the kitchen.

No, she would not take me to the doctor. It wasn't serious; it was all in my head, this feeling, this ache. She told me many times over the years that Father suffered intermittently from "spastic colon, the curse of the O'Briens," and she diagnosed me with it too, with a look of weary disappointment that I'd only ever seen before when I had finally convinced her that, like Father, I needed eyeglasses (my beloved baseball had become a blur). And here I was letting her down once more, with Paul overhead in the attic, bespectacled too, bedbound with his nameless despair.

"This is not the Danny I know," she said all summer long. "The Danny I know doesn't spend the day in bed. The Danny I know is healthy and strong."

When did I finally realize the cause? As she stood in my bedroom door and criticized, or said nothing as she bustled past in the hallway, her silence critical enough; I had only to think of her—not her words but her approaching presence—and her hands dug into my guts. No, not her hands but mine, my own mind.

That summer wore on and I was sick of being sick. I forced myself out of bed, ran shirtless through the village, wincing with every stride, trying to prove I was the "Danny" she knew; sprinting uphill and down beside the high school in the heat, mortifying my muscles with fatigue and my fair skin with sunburn, "It's Alright, Ma (I'm Only Bleeding)" in my headphones.

She requested—no, required—a research report for her and Father on the subject of how I planned to pay back the "investment" they were about to make in my college education. I went to the library, did my due diligence, and wrote the report, forecasting a job for myself four years from now in advertising or public relations, the only lucrative fields, she said, for "us creative types." I'd already agreed to attend a state school if the tuition was as prohibitive as she said it would be; I made her blink. She wanted me enrolled in that New England liberal arts college where the rich kids went. She needed the sticker on her station wagon. She needed the success of her children to demonstrate to her father and her family that her marriage hadn't been a failure.

I had assumed we would apply for financial aid, but Father refused, decrying the application process as an invasion of his God-given constitutional right to privacy. Many years later I'd learn that Grandpa Welsh was paying my tuition, as he'd done for Steven; possibly for Joyce too, and for Paul's only semester. So this was why my father said he didn't "give a shit" whether I went to college or not—"Move out and get a job!" he shouted one night, for all he cared.

At the end of the summer they drove me north into the Champlain Valley, with New York and the Adirondacks receding and the Green Mountains rising, to Middlebury College in Vermont. I was underweight, wrung out from the ache. We parked outside the dorm. In the twilight my mother handed me an almost empty box of supermarket cupcakes, as Father and my younger siblings waited in the car. That night I wrote a poem about missing them. My God—how could I? But the feeling, the ache, was gone.

For a time. Because the ache changed; now it was my ache alone and growing in me. I carried the ache with me, week-end nights down the snowing slope of the white chapel into Munroe Hall, and the empty classrooms with their empty wooden desks. Where I would sit and read and write while other students drank and fucked. I had never been so happy.

I paraded my ache in creative writing workshops, where a girl, who would soon become an editor at a prestigious Manhattan publishing house, honored me with an honest critique: "Your writing is crazy. Reading it makes me *feel* crazy. Is that what you want?" The answer was, then, yes.

Because I desired not only to write words but to live them, or to pretend to live them, my ache drew me inexorably into the theatre; where I was told I had a talent for losing my temper onstage; where I was cast often as afflicted royalty; where I found and fashioned families of artists with whom I could contend.

I wrote my first plays. Every audience was my mother and father, I'm embarrassed to admit. How the audience frustrated me with their stingy applause! If they applauded at all. Yet how desperately I desired more, while battering them with some "truth" they hadn't paid to hear, expecting scales to fall from their eyes, their stunned, admiring murmurs rippling toward the exits as the house lights rose.

Thus I was always failing; the ache begetting more ache . . .

If somebody in the audience knew me they might compliment me in the lobby, or at the bar afterward, by saying "You are nothing like your characters," or "*You* wrote this? I don't believe it." I'd feel perversely proud.

Instead of friends I filled my college years and my twenties with their simulacra as collaborators and colleagues. I required witnesses to my transfiguration, and I dressed the part: tatter-demalion thrift-store chic, scuffed combat boots, navy-blue pea coat, copious scarves. I acquired disciples, pseudofriends who would express their admiration—people who, for reasons unknown to themselves, needed heroes. I made enemies too: those who sensed my ache despite my strenuous performance of its absence.

I finished college at the top of my class, thanks to a course load of writing and acting, but also because I had flourished away from my family. I had resolved to prove them wrong: I wasn't like them. I would succeed, both for and in spite of them. In high school one of my more subtle acts of resistance had been to study rarely, if ever; in college I capitalized on their investment, but on my own terms. I delivered the graduating address in the chapel upon the hill, and the audience rose to their feet applauding. My parents, off to the side, were forced to rise too.

I was on my way to Ireland. I'd won a fellowship from the Thomas J. Watson Foundation, which provided me with enough money to survive a year on my own, conducting a course of "independent study" of Irish history and mythology and the theatre. My parents threw me a bon voyage party, a backyard cookout. They'd never hosted an adult celebration of any kind. Relatives I didn't recognize arrived—Great-Aunt Anne from Pearl River, and her middle-aged children with their spouses—all milling about our Weber grill in the torpor of a mid-August Saturday afternoon. Mother baked a vanilla sheet cake that Sally decorated with harps and shamrocks. That evening I lugged my backpack to the station wagon. Father said goodbye on the stoop: "It's only a year." We shook hands, and Mother drove me to JFK. Nobody said "I love you." I flew overnight. I'd never owned a passport before—never needed one—never crossed any ocean.

That foreshortened transatlantic night spilled me into the romance of my future. Sleep was elusive because superfluous. Peering through the porthole as we breached the coast: waves of fog dissipating above waves of sea breaking against cliffs; then fields so green they seemed to throb, interlaced every-where with violet stone walls like veins in the body of the earth—all of it just as I'd seen it in a prophesying dream many years before. I had believed in my escape so intensely for so long. We landed with a bump and applause.

Jumpy at passport control I declared my ache by explain-ing I was Irish, or Irish American, and bound to write a play (maybe even poetry!) about this country—"our country," I actually said—its history and myths and theatre. Entertained then annoyed then bored in an instant, the old man stamped my blank page. Outside I inhaled the native perfume: moss and coal, peat and stout. Reborn as I boarded a rickety bus at the airport in a bright wet dawn haze, as the driver, listening to Willie Nelson sing "On the Road Again," lurched us nau-seously toward Limerick.

It was the summer of Oasis; young men my age wore track suits exclusively. I told many of the Irish I met that I was "from the Bronx" before realizing I had neither the talent nor the dedication for the deception. I acted in amateur theatre productions in Cork and Belfast, a few times attempting their accents onstage; I won two minor prizes. I wrote plays and poems and rode more buses, slept on trains, on couches, in hostels; I went away with the fairies (and a conclave of Jungian storytellers) for a long weekend on cloudy Clear Island. I did what my family would never do, could never do—that's often how I chose precisely what to do—and what I did was as much for them as against them.

And every step of the journey my ache was with me. Pining for my future wife, back in Vermont, still in college, I discovered Nick Drake and Leonard Cohen. I spied my stubbled young face in transitory mirrors. I rented a narrow room in a flat on Pope's Quay in Cork, above the emerald-churning, malodorous Lee, a river rife with fiendish seagulls, oily swans, mangled supermarket trolleys revealed at low tide, and bloody-tongued drunks singing IRA songs along the quayside. My flatmate was the black-haired socialist son of Kerry cattle farmers; he had an incongruously East European accent, a missing front tooth, and the furtiveness of a serial killer (I never once saw the inside of his bedroom). Mad cow disease was all the rage and Connor the Kerryman wasn't buying it—the disease, that is: he bought meat all the time, enthused about the bargains. That winter and spring I shared a semidetached townhome in Salthill outside Galway with grad students who I overheard discussing in hushed tones one night the possibility of their new American housemate being "a bender." An attractive young chemist-in-training asserted that although, granted, I was a writer and—more incriminating still—a "man of the theatre," I could not be anything other than heterosexual because I listened to Tom Waits. (She was right: many evenings I walked the Salthill promenade in a spittle rain with several pints in my system, crying for my love far away, with *Closing Time* playing on my Walkman.) I got the flu, or it was depression. I prayed for time to pass and felt the guilt of that. I learned the medicinal value of whiskey. I flew home to JFK the following summer and took a train to grad school in Providence and I did not pay my taxes that year.

With the millennium I inserted myself into the

torrent of Manhattan and felt again spared, destined, heroic. Germophobic riding subways, holding fast to infectious poles and straps, living on next to nothing in a sublet in the East Village, three flights above an Irish pub, I wrote too many plays and not enough; saw some of my plays performed; taught aspirant playwrights for peanuts. I argued with my future wife, Jessica, the girl from college in Vermont, about whether or not I would "make it" as a writer—could I support her? A child? Children?—while working overnights as a computer clerk in an investment bank like the Doge's Palace, essentially a secretary for recently graduated frat brothers soon to ascend to their Scarsdale estates. If anybody asked me where I was from, if I had to answer, I would say: "The suburbs."

September 11th hit me on the sidewalk outside Jessica's sublet on Maiden Lane, papers cascading from the burning hole in the tower above, the second tower blooming black and red-gold before my eyes like an infernal rose. An old woman beside me simply sat down on the pavement, sobbing, "Oh no, oh no, oh no . . ." Joining the exodus through Chinatown, as bodies dropped from windows and the towers sank out of the sky, Jessica wept but I couldn't; I knew this was coming, some catastrophe like this, and I was ready. I deserved it: the curse of the O'Briens; or the curse of that day ending our youth, and the curse of the dust from the towers lingering in Jessica's apartment (we'd left her windows open) and causing or at least contributing to our coming cancers.

And still I carried my ache into my thirties. While friends foundered chartless upon the seas of themselves and their loves and careers, I steered an unwavering course, navigating by the pole star of my calling, feeling passive to a passion that was propelling me to London, Paris, Seville, Provence, Salzburg, Chiapas, Beijing, Jerusalem, the Arctic; not to mention

everywhere my words have borne me within the wide country of my own culture—Tennessee, Wisconsin, California . . .
This is bragging but self-astonishment too; as a child I feared
I would never be capable of leaving my home. And yet—here
(and there) I found myself again and again and again . . .

Then settling into the phantasmagoria of my middle years,
moving from New York to California, where my wife made
money as a television actor, and where the nearly impercep-
tibly changing seasons were blurring the years further. I sat
tethered to my desk, my ache like a cat in my lap, a freelancer
in flannels like my father before me, staring at a screen in an
upstairs room with the shades drawn low. Neighbors observed
me scowling in passing.

My wife and I fought more than many. We'd argue until she
cried; then I'd cry. She had a problem with anger, I told her. She
told me I was numb, too sensitive, my parents had abused me
so badly that I could not admit—could not see—how our war
of attrition was at least equally my fault. "There's something else
going on here," she insisted, time and again. Some ache that
was not hers. She gave herself migraines while I drank more.
Then running my many miles daily, as if I could absolve the
nights' bloat and carnage . . . And I was happy, escaping from
myself into this liquid slippage and an art where the ache in
my body of work might be cured. I found with relief that I
could no longer cry for myself; and when I did I cried for my
art, my rejection and inadequacy, my inevitable failure. All
of this fighting began around the time my parents disowned
me. When I started counting syllables again, that is, writing
poems, and plays in pentameter. When I grew a beard to hide
my ache but also to signal it. When I found a little writerly
success at last, or it found me. When I became with undeserved
joy a father.

And all the while I believed the ache was gone. That the ache was no ache at all. The ache was my purpose, and my purpose was to tell the truth, because the truth, when I found it and wrote it, would save me. And I still believe this.

But let me slow and reverse—to the break, the rupture; when in the midst of my striving I was surprised to receive, mere weeks before my wedding in 2006, an email:

> Dear Dan,
>
> Desperate move! When did you break faith with your dream of becoming a playwright?
>
> Love,
> Dad

A non sequitur surely. Some synaptic misfire. But the petty exclamation point was definitely his style. The "desperate move" referred, I could only speculate, to the fact that Jessica and I had decided to pay for our rehearsal dinner ourselves. He and Mother had offered (cheerlessly, as if fulfilling an unconscionable contract) to do so months before, but when the time came for planning the event they developed their usual paranoia. We were "taking them for granted," "taking advantage" of them because we'd wanted to add a few more guests to the list, like Jessica's aunt who was in treatment for a recurrence of ovarian cancer.

But that second sentence stung: "When did you break faith with your dream of becoming a playwright?" I hadn't broken any faith, hadn't abandoned my dreams. Did my father know something I didn't?

My younger brother Tom would tell me later on that our parents had been speculating around the dinner table, in the months before the wedding, that my soon-to-be father-in-law was leaning on me to relinquish my "dream of becoming a playwright" and go into business instead—his business, selling insurance. I hadn't "made it" as a writer; my plays had been performed "off-Broadway" my father explained to the family, "but not *on* Broadway."

He was confusing his story with mine. My fiancée's parents must have appeared affluent to him, with their woodland summer home in New Hampshire and a lakeside cocktail circle of friends. He was suffering a resurgence of the old inferiority he'd felt around my mother's family, the same humiliation that would make it intolerable for him and my mother and most of my siblings to attend our wedding.

The "love" in my father's signoff reads as it was intended: as its opposite.

He never wrote again—not even to show he cared enough to damn me, or to damn me further. He didn't call or send an email or message via surrogates nine years later, when he learned of my wife's cancer, then of my mine soon after.

How could this happen? Let me slow and reverse further, to the last time I saw my parents, when Jessica and I had driven from Manhattan to their new home in Charlottesville, Virginia. Tom was graduating from UVA; they'd moved with him four years earlier just as he enrolled, much to his consternation. He was their youngest so they must have been fearing the loss of him. It was also his birthday. And Paul was in the hospital in Westchester again, I learned from Tom, another suicide attempt, or ideation at least (my parents weren't sharing any details).

Father teased me that morning about my "hippie hair" (it

was curly and shaggy, a style seemingly de rigueur for adjunct professors of creative writing like me at the time), but there had been other warnings: Mother calling me repeatedly to complain about the difficulty of inviting relatives to our wedding, considering that her family hadn't spoken to her since she'd sued them, and Father's brothers John and Brian were disinterested and missing respectively. For the first time in my life I told her I was too busy to talk (or to listen). I was standing beside the fountain at Lincoln Center; I needed to go inside and watch some tape of an actor from a 1990s off-Broadway production. I was considering him for a play I had written about her, about our family but our family disguised.

At her request I had sent her the script months before. She said nothing about it until I inquired, when her response was only to ask, as ever, "But why does it have to be so sad?" Then Father had called, something he almost never did, and I answered, something I almost never did when their number popped up on my phone, one summer morning strolling along Bleeker Street in the Village where Jessica and I lived now and where they had never visited. He'd read my play too, he said. (He'd never read anything I wrote.) It was provocative, he said. Surely cosmopolitan New Yorkers would recognize its brilliance. Was he mocking me? Was he trying to show me that he couldn't be hurt by anything I had written—or would write—about him? Weeks later the play was panned. Although I didn't read any of the reviews, their existence would trouble me for years, the critics' rejection of my writing entangling hopelessly with my parents' rejection of me that afternoon at the end of May in Charlottesville.

I was sitting in a lawn chair in the backyard, freshly showered for dinner, while my sister Sally played in the grass with their new golden retriever. Father sank into the chair beside me. Sally with the puppy skulked away; the others vanished too, sensing a comeuppance, into the house, into bedrooms. Closing doors.

"What's wrong with you?" he asked. I couldn't respond. "There must be something terribly wrong," he said, "the way you look."

"How do I look?"

"Like you're homeless. Like you're insane." Like my brother Paul, was the implication; and—just like that—I was the family scapegoat.

He disapproved of my clothing. How insulting that I'd worn blue jeans to Tom's outdoor ceremony that day! It didn't matter that I was the only one who'd cheered for Tom, stood up to applaud as he received his diploma. Our parents had exited the quadrangle to answer a phone call from Paul, or to discuss what they were "going to do about Danny" (I would hear both explanations later from Tom).

And that long hair! that beard! It was disgusting and shameful, the way I looked.

"But this is how I dress—" I tried to defend myself. My tongue felt swollen, my limbs shrunken, my vision tunneling . . .

My treatment of my mother was unacceptable, he said. And here was the heart of it.

"What treatment?"

Again he said that something was obviously "terribly wrong" with me; my wedding was disturbing me, for reasons only I could understand. The insinuation was as mystifying as it was ugly. "We're taking a walk," he said, and stood.

"No."

"We're taking a walk—you and me." It was a threat.

I'd been to therapy, albeit only a few times. I stood up too: "I won't speak to you until you speak to me with kindness and respect."

Kindness and respect . . . Kindness and respect . . . How many times did I stammer my pathetic request?

He stepped closer. He was shorter than me—he'd been so since I was a teenager—and he shouted: "You have a problem with anger!"

"*I* do?"

"There are things you do not know!"

"About what?"

He repeated: "There are things you do not know!"

"Then tell me!"

But he wouldn't. Or couldn't. I retreated into the house and he pursued me. Mother swept down the stairs and clung to his side. "We're just being frank!" she cried. She seemed delighted, aroused even. They were happy, both of them giddy like they must have felt in their youth, rebelling against her family, eloping. I'd never seen them so in love before. And I felt in a flash that I knew what evil was. I'd always known it, but here it was unmasked.

Then again, bellowing: "There are things you do not know!"

Kindness . . . respect . . . my voice quavering, my finger quivering in his face. I could have knocked him flat, could've broken a chair or table with his bulk. I remembered the poet Robert Lowell, how he'd pushed his father down, how the old man's falling body shattered their "heirloom-clock, the phases of the moon, / the highboy quaking to its toes." How Lowell never recovered.

So I chose to save myself. Contain myself. In choosing to be kinder to him—than him—I might martyr myself; but I resolved that I would accept this gift.

Jessica came out of hiding and interrupted: "Today is not the day," she spoke firmly. This ought to be Tom's day, a day of celebration of his birth and his college degree, she scolded my parents, who stood there tongue-tied, bewildered. How could they be losing this fight? We escaped trembling by the back door. In our rental car, I knew it had happened, finally. It was over. I was free, or so I thought.

I was still carrying the old ache with me, in me, ten years later when I wandered groggily into our sun-suffused kitchen in Santa Monica the morning of September 11th—of all dates—and Jessica said, "Hey, feel this lump." I couldn't do it. I knew what was happening. I said simply, "Oh no, oh no, oh no," and sat down. Our daughter, not yet two years old, was eating red grapes.

Days later I was in Manhattan for auditions for a play of mine when a text from Jessica flashed on my phone: "It is cancer." The biopsy had confirmed it. The panic flushed my chest, neck, face, hands. I couldn't hear the actors saying my words. I couldn't tell any of my colleagues beside me in the rehearsal room. What I could do was hurry to a taxi to the airport and cry behind my sunglasses behind the departure monitors. The flight was unbearable. How did I pass the time? How did I stand or speak to Jessica when I opened the door to our home that night? How did we sleep?

We got on with it: the double mastectomy and breast reconstruction; the egg harvestings and fertilizations that failed; the months of chemotherapy through the long fall into winter. When I wasn't caring for Jessica and our daughter I would sometimes dine out alone, drinking too much. I was angry: of course this would happen to me, the constant caretaker again, as I had been all my life, first for my mother. I was the stoic, meant to see her through. And I would see Jessica through. Despite my fear and self-pity at moments, I knew this was the role I was born to play.

She wore a helmet of ice packs during infusions so that she might keep her hair; she hoped to keep working, if she could, but more importantly we wanted to shield our daughter from the worst of it. She wore ice mittens and ice slippers to stave off neuropathy, but also to retain her fingernails and toenails, and an ice mask for her lashes and brows. Weekly I'd sit beside my mummified wife, inserting crackers into her mouth, a bendy straw for sparkling water, while reading to her aloud (and loudly, to penetrate the helmet) from *Real Simple*, *Coastal Living*, while tubes were seeding her blood with the molecules that would scour and perhaps save her body; while around us patients reclined in varying stages of panic and despondency, gray-faced, some cadaverous. Curtains were drawn yet we heard their moaning, weeping, begging. We did the same behind our curtains.

And meanwhile my ache was growing. I had understood "the curse of the O'Briens" as a manifestation of stress, and these were undeniably stressful times. I was tired, but we were new parents. I denied the severity of my symptoms. And what were the chances of two cases of cancer in the same family in the same year? Perversely I was welcoming my pain, a masochistic form of empathy, as if I were willing myself to suffer with my wife to the point of bleeding. But the cramping grew insufferable. When I woke from twilight sedation the gastroenterologist said he couldn't get the scope "in there," the tumor was too large.

I would be diagnosed with stage 4 colon cancer with metastasis to the liver. Luckily—I want to say miraculously—the metastasis consisted of two small lesions located in a "resectable" portion of my liver. I was given a decent chance for a cure. My liver surgeon told me that five years ago I would have been given only months to live.

But first they would have to excise seven inches of my descending colon, along with ten percent of my bladder, for safe measure. Then I'd receive four months of intense chemotherapy—they would "hit me with everything," was how my oncologist put it, because I was relatively young and could withstand it. Then my liver would be resected, about fifteen percent of it cut out. They'd remove my gallbladder too—again, just to be safe. Then two more months of chemo. My treatment, they promised, would be over by Christmas.

My formal diagnosis came on the day of Jessica's final chemotherapy infusion. She arrived at my oncologist's examination room, just down the corridor from her oncologist's office, unsteady on her feet and still wearing her helmet of ice, her last infusion still pumping through her veins. Because my colon was almost entirely blocked by the tumor, my surgery would be an emergency. Jessica laughed through her tears: I was stealing her spotlight, she said.

I woke up from the anesthesia to discover my belly stapled from pubis to navel. At first I was conscious of every breath like a cool drink of water—breaths like sips that might keep me alive. "Now take a deep breath," said a nurse. "Now take a few steps." When I tried to take those first few steps I swooned into the nurse's arms.

Three days passed before a young doctor suggested, "Here, drink some water. Try some juice." But my colon must have been leaking because I started throwing up black bile and spiked a fever of a hundred and four. My wife fainted. I don't recall a lot. It could have been the Dilaudid, but every time I closed my eyes I saw people at my bedside, some speaking to me: "Hello." People not actually there: "What's your name?" Strangers, and my mother asking: "Why can't you tell me, Danny? Why does it always have to end so sad?"

I begged my wife to make sure that my name had been left off the registry, but I needn't have worried. No family showed up, called, emailed, texted. As everybody knows, the gravely ill often call out for their mothers, which only seems natural, but I felt no such urge. Opening my eyes I saw the hospital room; closing them I saw travelers whirling around as if we were in Grand Central Station. Some stopped to notice me. They looked curious, confused.

The nurses shoved a tube up my nose—"Hold still"—and down into my stomach to drain the bile. Gagging—"Hold him"—struggling in their arms—"Breathe in." My surgeon arrived, munching on a nutrition bar. His name sounded alarmingly like Kevorkian. He was inclined to cut again. See what was happening inside.

"It's a toss-up," he said.

"I just need more time," I said weakly, "to heal."

"Your choice."

I chose to wait and see, and I got lucky. Once a day Jessica led me shuffling through the halls of the hospital, my ass winking out of my gown, pushing my tree of IVs, piss-bag dangling too, taking in the views of the frat houses of UCLA, cars, palm trees, celluloid sun. It was Good Friday when they'd operated on me, which is good news from a certain point of view. Then thirteen days in the hospital. My lucky number, I used to believe, because February 13th was the date my brother tried to kill himself, and he'd survived.

Why us? I'm sure I will wonder as long as I am able. We exercised, bought organically at farmers markets. I'd been a dedicated hand-washer all my life. Neither of us smoked. Was I too moody, pessimistic? Superficially, maybe, but would I have ever written a single word without some core conviction that communication, that hope, is possible? And stress—who's not stressed? And what constitutes stress? The stress of publishing a book or premiering a play? These things should hardly count.

Was this my family's punishment for leaving them behind? I'd had no choice; they left me, or they forced me to leave them. But it's one of the Ten Commandments: obey one's mother and father. Had I angered God, or the cosmos? Did I smite myself subconsciously with my guilt? Had I worked myself to death, or close to it? Had I professed a belief in the transcendent power of literature and theatre while shellacking my resentments into the black pearl of a tumor?

Had I been too happy without my old family, too happy with my new? Was this the price my wife and I had to pay for the unaccountable windfall of our daughter?

I'll never know. Like the circumstances of a birth and the events of an upbringing, the fact and story of my illness is chaotic, mostly accidental, and meaningless save for the meaning I find myself striving to make with these words. "Don't ask 'Why me?'" a surgeon advised me early on. "Ask 'Why *not* me? Why not any of us?'"

And what of my family? The family I escaped, not the family I've made. Have I forgotten them? Evidently not; though remembering them doesn't trouble me like it used to. I have enjoyed writing every word of this. Have I forgiven them? If forgiveness is understanding then this book is my attempt.

They have let me go—I don't hear from them. I'm no longer pursued or buried alive in my dreams. The cancers silenced them, having frightened or shamed them. Sometimes during the long months of chemotherapy I wanted them to care, to send a greeting card, to apologize; one night I dreamed of my mother soothing me, stroking my hair as I laid my head in her lap, as I'd never done in life. But an illness like cancer clarifies. When you or a loved one are gravely ill, you cannot help but feel that now is undeniably, inescapably now. Nothing matters aside from doing everything you can—and then some—to keep her alive, to keep yourself alive. So pain of any kind, and the people that inflict pain, are less compelling to me now. I want to live; I feel freer. So this book's conclusion is my farewell to them. My hope is that now the cancer is gone, and with it the ache of my childhood.

1986 / 1996 / 2006 / 2016

THERE IS ONLY one story left to tell: the happy ending of my childhood. It begins four times, every ten years.

1986 was boom and bust for my father: his son had tried to kill himself that winter, but by summer he was driving a new car down our dead-end street where we played baseball with a tennis ball. We leapt onto the curb and the dog-soiled grass to clear the way for him. Then behind him, pursuing the silhouetted dome of his baldness, his thick hands upon the wheel, ten and two, I skipped, tossing my sunny dusty sphere into the air. He stepped from the car, loafers grinding our gravel, pulling his tie loose and swinging his blazer over his shoulder like a TV commercial.

In his new Cutlass Ciera four-door sedan, corporate gray, a dignified pin-thin racing stripe in red along its flanks, burgundy leather interior, power windows, digital tuner and cassette player: our father had arrived.

In retrospect the Ciera was not so impressive. What did the name mean anyway? A homonym of *Sierra* as in Mountains? And a cutlass like, what, a pirate's saber? That bar of flags like a military ribbon on the driver's side imparted the car with a stodgy patriotism that suited my father well. Soon we were calling the Cutlass the Gutless—behind his back, of course—due to its timid four cylinders, its feeble front-wheel drive, and its overcautious driver too.

Ten years later he gave me his car, or lent it to me, rather. I was skeptical. It was my last year at college, and he and Mother knew I'd be leaving soon—as soon as I could, I would flee as far as I could; they seemed to believe that his car might keep me closer to home. That winter he'd been named the executor of his father-in-law's estate ("Because we knew he needed the money, and just to give him something to *do*," his stepmoth-er-in-law Regina told me years later). So he bought himself a burgundy-colored Volvo, and his old Gutless, its rust spots plastered over with metallic duct tape, was mine to drive back to Vermont, where I took my future wife on our first date, embarrassed by its malfunctioning passenger seat because if she leaned back even slightly she'd find herself sinking into a near-supine position. This had been my plan all along, she joked. As long as I'd known her, a year or so, we couldn't stop each other from laughing.

We drove slowly through a twilight snowstorm to the restaurant of an inn where I confessed my childhood, as I understood it then; and she didn't recoil. Over greasy chicken sandwiches in wax-paper-lined baskets, the tabletop votives around us like jewels, she confessed much the same. Ten years later we would marry.

That night I drove her back to her dorm and parked, and she got out. I could have let her walk into the black trees and the blue snow beneath the white moon; just as I could have surrendered when, twenty years later, she was diagnosed with cancer, and then after six months I was too. Instead I followed her into the night and turned her around with the sound of my voice calling her name.

Then driving up the mountain to the cabin I shared with friends in Ripton, my father's car sliding, slicing along harrowing cliffside bends, beside the frozen skin of a river trickling within—I felt exultant, as if I'd found myself improbably the inheritor of my father's vast fortunes.

Then climbing the stairs. The tall arc of her back in the old bed in the cold house. Clinging to her side for my life—I knew it already. Embers were glowing in the grate of the wrought-iron stove; snow billowed against the windows and black flies hatched in the walls and mice filled the pockets of our discarded clothes with seeds.

In the morning Jessica opened her eyes, in the clear winter light, with that obliterating smile our daughter now smiles that asks, *What's next?*

Coda

SEVEN YEARS HAVE passed. Somehow we're still alive. My brother Paul has died; the cause is undetermined. The super found him on the floor of his bathroom in his apartment in Scarsdale. No note; a heart attack or stroke, I'm told. He was fifty-three.

My daughter will turn ten this year. I imagine the memoir she may one day write about me, about her mother, about growing up here in California. I hope she never feels the need. I hope her childhood has been and will be boring, unencumbered, defined by love, and harrowing only in the mundane, necessary ways. I hope she will forgive me as I have forgiven my family.

For a long time I put this memoir aside. I wrote it when I thought I was dying, and when I didn't—well, I didn't know how the story should end. Now I know it should end because my life hasn't. These memories of my childhood are fading, my cancer scars are fading; my brother is at rest. Last summer in the ocean my daughter noticed the long scar in my abdomen and asked, "What happened?" I hadn't told her yet; I won't do that to her until I have to. "It's nothing," I said. "It was something that had to be taken out of me, a long time ago." She smiled. "I'm glad," she said, and turned to swim for the shore.

Acknowledgments

An earlier version of a section of this book was published with the title "Dear Brother" in the *New England Review* Vol. 40, No. 2 (2019). My thanks is due to Editor Carolyn Kuebler and Nonfiction & Drama Editor J.M. Tyree.

My thanks to Chad W. Post, Will Evans, Walker Rutter-Bowman, Sara Balabanlilar, Kaija Straumanis, Anna Jordan, and all at Dalkey Archive Press and Deep Vellum.

And lastly my thanks to the many who have helped over the years with encouragement, insights, and suggestions, none more consistently and sympathetically than Jessica St. Clair.

Printed in the USA
CPSIA information can be obtained
at www.ICGtesting.com
JSHW020746200923
48752JS00004B/5